NEANDE

THE EXPERIMENT

BY

SERAG MONIER

NEANDERTHALS:

THE EXPERIMENT

BY

SERAG MONIER

Copyright © 2021 Serag Monier

All rights reserved. No part of this book may be reproduced or used in any manner without the prior written permission of the copyright owner, except for the use of brief quotations in a book review.

This is the English translation of the Arabic novel ذ ياذدرة ال التجربة originally published in Egypt in 2020 by Al Kotob Khan. http://www.kotobkhan.com

First edition April 2021

Translated by Eman Thabet
Edited by Susan Uttendorfsky
    www.adirondackediting.com
Cover art by Mohammed A. Mosilhy
Layout by Susan Uttendorfsky

Cover photo: @bobby_hendry © 2013, 2021 on Unsplash.com

This book is a work of fiction. Any references to historical events, real people, or real places are used fictitiously. Other names, characters, places, and events are products of the author's imagination, and any resemblance to actual events or places or persons, living or dead, is entirely coincidental.

i

Dedication

To My Mother, Hajja Sa'adat Altantawy

Table of Contents

Dedication iii
1 1
2 5
3 14
4 21
5 28
6 36
7 43
8 51
9 58
10 66
11 74
12 79
13 88
14 98
15 105
16 114
17 123
18 131
19 139

20	146
21	156
22	165
23	173
24	181
25	189
26	196
27	206
28	213
29	222
30	230
31	238
32	247
33	258
Epilogue	267
Author Biography	272

1

I sprinted aimlessly, breathless and running out of strength, but I didn't have the luxury to choose otherwise. My feet raced as I stepped on broken tree branches, odd-colored puddles, and reeking animal dung, while my face kept clashing into overhanging tree branches. I had no idea where I was, what chased after me, or where I was headed.

***

The only possible explanation at the time was that I was dreaming. They say a dream can be so vivid it can deceive you. But how could I wake up to find myself sleeping on the ground in the woods? There aren't any forests in Egypt, and I only left Egypt once in my life anyway. When I woke up, the smell of animal dung filled my nose, but it was also mixed with a sturdy smell—similar to that of glue, which some find addictive. My cheek rested on a dry branch and I was surrounded by trees with dusty-blue–colored leaves. Their branches extended from the lowest part of the stems up to almost three meters high, and then the leafless boughs themselves stretched up to a high distance—like mambo trees.

Because I thought I was dreaming, I closed my eyes for a second in hopes of the dream coming to an end, but soon enough I felt a nose sniffing my face. I cowered in fear and disgust when a slippery tongue licked my forearm. I swiftly pulled away and opened my eyes only to find a wolf, or a large dog, with pied yellowish skin, curiously watching me. It stepped back when I opened my eyes, but it kept walking around me in circles while fixing its gaze upon me. I reached out to grasp anything nearby to hit it with, but only found a small stick that I threw at it, making it take a small step back.

It then looked up to the sky and let out a strange, shrill howl. Only few seconds later, several howls echoed from a distance and it became obvious that the wolf viewed me as a meal to be shared with its pack. As soon as I realized that, I leaped up and sprinted away as fast as I could. It immediately began to chase after me, running casually! It didn't try to hunt me down, indicating that it actually enjoyed the chase.

No, it wasn't a dream. I became certain at this point. My heart pounded and my face burned from all the wounds I sustained from those strange trees and their intermingling branches. The word "branches" lit up in my head, and I realized they were the answer...

I climbed the boughs of the first large tree I encountered. I remembered that thirty years ago I used to climb sycamore and mulberry trees, but I wasn't that strong anymore. I continued to climb until I was fairly distant from the ground. The animal remained down there, standing. It wasn't trying to climb and it didn't look like it could.

I caught my breath, still keeping my eye on the animal, and tried to recall what happened: *How did I end up here?*

A few minutes later, the animal (allow me to call it "the wolf" to make things easier) was still waiting when a pack of four wolves showed up and joined the original one waiting under the tree. There was no clue what language they used to communicate. The first one didn't make a sound, but they all looked up at me. After that, the largest member of the pack approached the trunk below the branch I was seated on, sniffed it, then walked back, snarling. The five began to bark in my direction in a crescendo that implied hostility—as though the biggest one viewed me as a dangerous enemy, not just a meal.

My head almost exploded as I remained seated on the branch, watching the wolves bark at me. I considered if they were dogs, but then I remembered their howling and assumed again that they were wolves. Their barking resembled hostile cursing, and I sat there in panic, clueless to as to what brought me to that place or how to escape it.

At the time, all I thought about was, *How long am I going to remain stuck here while these monsters anticipate my fall?* I then reassured myself: *At least things can't get any worse!*

I was proven wrong. The wolves approached the tree. Each one held on to a branch, and they all began to move it aggressively together. Their extreme strength made the tree actually start to shake, with me on it and almost falling from terror.

I was desperately holding on to the branch with my right hand when my attention suddenly shifted to some fruit hanging among the tree limbs. They looked like doum fruit,[1] about the size of a volleyball. I grabbed one and it felt hard, so I pulled it off and violently threw it on one of the wolves' head. It howled in pain and quit pulling at the branch. Encouraged, I repeated the action until they all somewhat backed off...just as my supply of fruit was running out. One carefully approached the tree. When I didn't throw anything at it, it grabbed on to the tree once again, followed by the rest. They began to shake the tree more aggressively than before.

I tried to climb to a higher branch so I could grab more fruits to throw at them: desperate attempts by a trapped rat, one that has no idea if its life will be saved or left to fate! I picked a fruit and threw it strongly at the alpha wolf at the same moment I was trying adjust my position. The action threw me off balance and ultimately made me fly through the air, landing among them in immobility.

---

[1] *Hyphaene thebaica:* A hard brown fruit grown on a special type of palm trees common in Egypt.

2

The fall was gentler than expected...

The ground was soft, and my desperate efforts to grab on to branches right before falling down made the situation slightly better. Those attempts didn't succeed in preventing me from falling as much as they succeeded in ripping the skin of my arm. After I landed, blood was dripping down my right arm from a long wound that extended from my forearm all the way to my wrist. It wasn't that deep, but it was definitely more than a simple scratch.

I didn't pay much attention to the wound, for I was about to be devoured by some strange-looking animals I'd never seen before. The five began to sniff and surround me as I lay helplessly on the ground. I readjusted my arm, which made one of them growl at me, encouraging me to lie entirely still. Maybe it was a species that shunned human flesh, and they only besieged me because they thought I was some threat to be dealt with.

One approached my wounded arm with its snout and stuck its tongue out to lick the line of dripping blood, then proceeded to raise its head up to the sky and howl. Then it stepped aside. The second one came along, waited until more blood formed on my arm, licked it, howled, and stepped aside. The others followed the same exact procedure as I remained motionless. Their act was similar to a ritual performed by a primal tribe rather than the behavior of a group of wild animals.

At that moment, I again became sure I was dreaming. I thought that after I woke up, I would call a dream-interpretation TV show and the interpreter would say something along the lines of:

"Those wolves represent the lusts that consume you, and their licking of your blood indicates their desired consumption of your soul itself."

> Lust of the flesh, money, possession, and all that meaningless talk. This extremely vivid dream may even be a sign of mental illness.
>
> If I visited a psychiatrist, he'd assure me that the wolves symbolized deeply rooted issues in my life. One wolf, for instance, represents my math teacher, who despised me for three whole years, beating me in every class. I am unspeakably blockheaded with numbers, but I never took a private class with him, unlike the other similarly afflicted students who wanted to prevent his nastiness. My dad believed that teachers who beat their students practiced a positive and noble act, but it never occurred to him that it can sometimes be an act of sadism and catharsis.
>
> Another wolf would be Hashim, the swindler who stole five years' worth of my savings and sent me off to Abu Dhabi, where I realized my work contract with him was a

scam. I returned home with absolutely nothing.

As for the largest wolf, that one surely represents my constant lack of satisfaction with my career, despite how well my job pays. After all, it is sufficient enough for my daily needs, my failed marriages, and my obscure writings. That wolf may also depict my despair about my college degrees—which aren't doing much for me—and my eternal loneliness in a life with no wife or kids.

But could the psychiatrist justify how the wolves don't look like real wolves? Their long and narrow snouts, short ears, and multi-colored skin—similar to that of tigers... They sometimes howl with a quality of shrillness, and other times bark as if they were coughing. The doctor would claim it is an outcome of my unstable sense of imagination, which is being influenced by my psychological state...

Back in the real world, this situation would definitely be a dream.

It was suppertime and the wolves were ready to tear at my flesh. The alpha began to approach me, saliva dribbling down its snout, but it stopped when another pack of wolves suddenly emerged from a cluster of shrubs that I hadn't stepped into yet. Without any buildup, a fight began.

The other pack consisted of three sand-colored wolves with no spots on their bodies, but their sizes were larger than the pack that had already detained me. The alpha wolf from the first group attacked the smallest one in the latter, then each pair from my pack (Yes, I can call them *my pack*, as they all licked my blood) charged the other two remaining from the second group. It appeared to be a preplanned event. The battle turned fiercer and different types of howls were released into the air: some were howls of pain, some were crying out for help, and others were deliberately scary.

I began to crawl away, with my hands still on the ground and my eyes fixated on them. The largest wolf from my pack was almost beating his rival.

My hand encountered a lever in the trunk of the tree I escaped to earlier. I grabbed it and tried to pull it. It moved in its place but soon went back to its position, as if shut with a spring. I yanked it one more time and it produced a loud noise that made both wolf packs stop fighting and freeze. They all began to bark while slowly moving toward me. I shook the handle some more and it opened, and I realized it was a door to what appeared to be a tunnel or an underground room. Consequently, I quickly threw myself in, the door shut itself after I entered, and then I was swallowed by the dark.

I remained still for a few minutes while hearing them bark and scratch at the ground outside. My eyes gradually became accustomed to the darkness and revealed a tunnel, which I threw myself in. It was spacious: higher than two meters and almost two and a half meters wide. It stretched a long way ahead, with little holes in its ceiling that allowed the light in. It smelled rotten, like a stagnant pond, and

I was getting so thirsty that my throat clenched in dryness. I felt the walls and touched some waterdrops, reminding me of seepage that leaked from a broken pipe. It occurred to me to lick the drops on the wall, but the idea made me nauseous. I decided to wait in hopes of finding a different water source. I walked for a few short meters before my strength ran out completely, forcing me to sit on the ground and rest my exhausted body.

I pushed myself and attempted to lick the liquid off the wall before spying a part of the ceiling where water regularly dripped. I walked with difficulty toward it and sat underneath with my mouth up and open, swallowing one drop after the other. I wasn't paying much attention to the concerns in my head about the water source or its questionable taste.

I began to acknowledge I wasn't dreaming, breaking out of my denial zone. I was in a forest, being chased by wild animals from which I was hiding in a tunnel, drinking filthy water. Starving and feeling excruciating pain from wounds on my legs, face, and forearm, I tried to recall the events from the previous day—my last memory from the real world, filled with car noises and human battles.

***

I remember waking up and heading to a residential compound, whose owners I contract with to carry out weekly plumbing maintenance work.

I own a store that sells plumbing materials and bathroom accessories. My work is rewarding, and I can show off my money to my hometown peers to compensate for the things my life lacks, which their lives don't. For instance, each one has a family and children—unlike me, who has decided to never have kids.

I was married twice. Each time I chose a wife, I made it clear that I didn't want to have kids, to which they both initially agreed. The first one was already a mother, and the second married me at an older age...and was not by all means attractive. But because women quickly forget their promises when they have to do with their maternal instincts, both my first and second wife reneged on their promises and insisted having children, so divorces took place.

On that previous morning, I pass by all the water sprinklers that irrigate landscapes. I fix a fountain, correct some pool pumps, and repair other plumbing issues here and there. Work is abundant and never-ending, the compound manager is extremely gullible, and most of the women who live in these compounds are catty and repulsive. A few are attractive, and some walk by in revealing clothes, but I'm used to viewing them as objects. I never even think about sneaking a peek—not because of noble morals, but because the women don't excite me to the extent that I would risk losing such a financially rewarding contract.

At night I stay in my store for around an hour, then leave it to my assistant and head to a literary session. I spend time with some obscure writers, like myself, in a coffeehouse in Abbassia. I pay for the drinks, as usual, since I am the richest and the only one who never complains about manual labor. I've also left the traditional governmental jobs they still occupy.

The day before I woke in this strange place was ordinary, just like any other day. My memory doesn't provide any clue about what I'm going through at the moment. I think about the reason I'm here as the smell of the tunnel's filth fills my nostrils. I tell myself: *Maybe I'm kidnapped and some mad scientists are conducting an experiment on me. I may've lost all my memories and forgotten events from whole years in my life, during which perhaps I traveled and worked as drug or arms dealer with a Colombian drug cartel. Then I had an accident that erased all my memories.*

In any case, I am going to die either from starvation or a severe case of stomach virus based on the filthy water I'm filling my tummy with. The world is going to miss a renowned drug dealer like the one I might be.

Yes, it must have been one of the compound's villa owners where I work. Someone persuaded me to work with him, and it seems as though I am too good at my job. He sent me out to more missions in Colombia. The plane carrying the drugs crashed and fell in this forest. And that's how I lost five years' worth of memories...

I smile in relief at the appealing idea. Drug dealing doesn't do much harm, except to the addicts, and it's not the most malevolent act in the world if you compare it to the evil that all world governments direct toward their people, and those from different countries.

I admire my philosophy more than the idea with which I'm attempting to explain my current situation.

***

I tried to doze off. For few minutes I remained still, with my eyes closed, attempting to push away all the persistent thoughts. Abruptly I twitched with goosebumps when I sensed something crawling up my body. I kicked my leg aggressively and saw a medium-sized snake slamming into the wall in front of me. Then it walked toward me again.

Yes, walked. The snake displayed tiny legs all over its torso—similar to centipedes, but the legs were underneath the snake instead of on its sides.

It moved faster than regular snakes, reaching me in less than two seconds and stinging me. I kicked it even harder, then held it from the center of its body and smacked its head violently against the wall until it quit moving. I held it up quickly and peered at its fangs to check whether it was the poisonous kind. I was ignorant when it came to snakes, but I remembered watching some folks in a show doing that.

I couldn't understand its mouth structure, and my panic increased when I felt some sort of pain spreading from the bite mark to my upper thighs. I rolled up my pants and scrutinized the fang marks, finding blisters spreading on my leg, and I was soon overwhelmed by an itchy feeling. I accepted my destiny, laid down, and told myself that its venom was starting to work. Half an hour passed and nothing happened except for the stubborn itch, as though the snake bestowed a bee's effect instead of venom.

I dozed off once more after the itch calmed down, and when I woke up, all I had in mind was hunger. I thought about heading back to the tunnel's gate and climbing out once more to search for fruit that was good to eat. I didn't remember noticing any fruit other than the hard ones I threw at the wolves.

I scolded myself out loud to pull myself together and I attempted to get up. When my hand leaned on the snake in this attempt, it occurred to me to eat it. Skin it first, then consume its raw flesh, as we used to do in "thunderbolt forces" during my obligatory military service back in my twenties. I didn't hesitate very long and was beginning to prepare my meal when I suddenly heard a woman screaming from the other end of the tunnel.

3

Ehab shut down his laptop while remaining seated next to Omar—a patient in the critical burn unit—as soon as Dr. Hend entered the room. The doctor stood firmly and gazed at her patient, lying in bed, declaring that time was up and she had gone too easy on him. He looked at her imploringly.

She responded, attempting to resist her compassion toward him. "You've been telling Ehab your story for two hours. You've delayed your mealtime and your wound dressing."

He raised his gauze-wrapped arm, attempting to make a bargain. He offered to drink an entire glass of milkshake mixed with eggs in exchange for Ehab writing one more page for him before he got up and accompanied her for the dressing.

Omar arrived at the hospital around a month ago, suffering from critical burns caused by unknown means. They were mysterious-looking wounds that Hend had never encountered before, spread all over Omar's body in a way that indicated a stream of flame broke out from the ground beneath him, striking his lower limbs, the sides of his torso, and his arms.

Time after time she inquired how he acquired those wounds, but he never gave her an answer. After a two-week fever that almost killed him, he decided to finally reveal the secret behind his injuries, but insisted that the story must be written down for the world to know.

He was accompanied by Ehab, his plumbing store's assistant's brother. Omar paid him to write for a few hours a day. After reading the first chapters of his story, it occurred to Hend that possibly he was experiencing hallucinations from burn toxins that reached his brain.

She wanted a mental health professional to visit Omar. Since her hospital didn't have a psychiatry department, she called Abbassia Psychiatric Hospital, asking them to send a doctor for him. Unfortunately, they told her a psychiatrist wouldn't be available for at least three days.

Omar held the milkshake in his hand and contemptuously but rapidly drank it, complaining that the liquid's inclusion of eggs made the milkshake taste staler than stinky salted fish. Before leaving him to continue the story, Hend called for the nurse to attach a fresh bag of the IV solution, the tube for which ran into a vein in Omar's neck.

Ehab sat on a chair by his bed in the intensive care room, which currently held another patient separated from him by a thick gray curtain. The electric bed was the only thing that worked in the entire room: Next to his bed was a broken monitor and a ventilator, waiting in anticipation for its turn to end his life. Ehab lifted the laptop's lid again, re-opened the writing file, and then Omar continued telling his story in a weary voice.

**

The woman called out for help using clear Egyptian words. Her voice sounded so close that it made me think the tunnel was short, possibly not extending beyond ten meters. Then I realized her voice was actually coming from a door in the ceiling, after which the tunnel stretched an unknown distance. The door was so high my hands could barely reach it, even when I jumped as high as I could. So how was I to open it? The woman persistently screamed and cried for help. Her shrieks clouded my thoughts as I looked around, trying to find a way to climb up to the door.

I slid my hands against the walls beneath the door in different directions, hoping to find a ladder or any sort of protrusion to hang on to—and the woman wouldn't stop screaming! *Her hysteria is going to make me leave her to become a meal for the wolves*, I thought. It actually occurred to me for a moment to leave her, as I might get up there to save her and just get killed instead.

No, no one is getting killed!

I decided that when I opened the door slightly, I would signal her to run so she could come and hide with me. A speedy, practical, and safe plan! Moreover, I was not staying there forever, so there had be a way for me to get out of that tunnel.

I finally felt some steplike bulges that reached the door. I grabbed on to a high step that was slippery, but I held on tightly and began to climb. The woman let out another loud scream, which startled me. My hands let go and I fell to the ground, cursing women altogether and cursing my bad luck in being in a strange forest with a woman who wouldn't stop shrieking.

I gathered my strength once more and made another attempt until I was able to reach the door. I carefully pushed it with my right hand while my left hand grabbed onto a knob by the door. I saw her, but didn't catch much of her facial features. Her attire, though, was more than ordinary: loose black pants, a long olive-colored blouse that reached all the way to her thighs, and a green headscarf with different colored ribbons attached to it.

She stood on a branch and underneath her were ten large rats, the size of cats, waiting. As soon as she caught sight of me, she called out for help, begging me to shoo them away. I didn't move. I only impatiently signaled that she should join me—without saying a word. I didn't want the rats to shift their attention to me.

She waved her arms again and called out, and when she saw me only gesturing at her, she shouted in irritation, "Get a grip! Be a man!"

I secretly cursed her, but she had a point. They were nothing but rats, and I could chase them away to save her. In addition, her screaming would attract the wolves' attention, and that was the last thing I needed. I crammed my head and arms between the door opening and the ground, then raised my body to exit the tunnel. I yelled at the rats. As expected, the sound made them move toward me, so I picked up a solid branch from the ground and waved it at them until they scattered.

I headed toward the woman and reached out my arm to pat her on the shoulder, but she leaped down and grabbed me by the collar, demanding to know who I was and how I had brought her to that place. I tried to calm her but she kept on blabbering, claiming she had been abducted and that I was the one behind it. It seemed obvious that she was in shock. I tried once more to calm her down, but she pushed me away and sat on the ground to cry.

I let her be until she began to collect herself; then I approached and assured her that I was in the same exact situation. I went to sleep and woke up the next morning to find myself in this forest. She insisted that I explain it, but I asked her to join me in the tunnel first and continue our conversation there before the wolves returned. She looked at me suspiciously and asked about the tunnel, and how I found out about it. I told her my story, but she refused to join me, with an attitude that implied I was inviting her to my own place.

I swore that I was well-intentioned and that I was terrified of what we might encounter in the woods, but she still firmly refused. I let her know there was water down there, and a freshly-slaughtered, peeled snake ready to be eaten, but the idea made her nauseous and she declined. Nothing could persuade her to come down with me... Except the nearby sound of wolves howling.

She walked behind me hurriedly until we reached the door, but when I grabbed the knob to open it, it wouldn't cooperate. My face went pale and I felt anxious, trying again and again while she watched me impatiently, but it still wouldn't open. She shivered in panic when the howling escalated. I looked around to spot the door into which I originally entered. All the trees looked the same and the passages between them were identical. I froze, so she inquired what the tunnel and door looked like and what the handle's direction was, so I understood what she meant. She was intelligent and quick on her feet, despite what her constant screaming earlier implied.

Keeping the direction of the handle and tunnel in mind, I was able to guess which passage we were supposed to walk through. I grabbed her hand and quickly headed toward it, but she yanked her hand away and insisted she was going to walk behind me, with no need for me to drag her by the hand. I walked rapidly in front of her, mumbling irritably about her inflexibility. The howling was approaching when she stopped me to state we'd walked more than twenty meters, so we probably already missed the door.

I stood in confusion, looking in both directions until I finally spotted the correct tree. We ran toward it, but when I looked at the ground, I found the doorknob broken. I tried to pull it by its remains, but it slipped from my hand while the howling increased and the wolves approached.

I thought of no other option but to climb the tree once more and wait until they left. When I shared the idea with her, she heatedly insisted they were going to follow our smell. I assured her that my blood was still fresh and would cover our natural odor. I helped her get up while she remained grumpy. As I expected, the two wolves walked away, probably heading to find another meal. She looked at me and asked if we should get back down, but I told her to wait a little bit more until they were completely out of sight.

She ignored me and climbed down anyway and fell to the ground clumsily. She wasn't that heavy, but was chubby enough so her waistline was unidentifiable, making her torso appear as one piece, with no curves at all. She rested on the ground to catch her breath and tell me the story of how she found herself there.

4

She was shivering as she spoke, but I was hesitant to console her physically so she wouldn't scold me again. She didn't say much about herself at first. She only mentioned she had been in an elevator that suddenly started to shake vigorously, and her head hit one of its walls. She passed out and woke up to find herself in the forest. She remained motionless and in shock for a while, trying to grasp what had happened. She didn't think it was a dream, like I did. She thought that she'd been kidnapped for a reason she didn't understand.

She heard the howling sounds from time to time, which was another reason she froze in place. But when she saw the large rats, they drove her to run nonstop until she ran out of breath. Then the rats surrounded her at the bottom of the tree.

I asked if it was possible that she lost her memories and that a number of years had been erased from her mind. She looked at me belittlingly and showed me marks on her forearm, claiming she acquired them the day before arriving, when she was preparing dinner.

She mentioned that she was dying of thirst, so I told her about the water in the tunnel. She rejected the idea and suggested we look for a clean source of water, claiming that since water was leaking in the tunnel, that must mean that there was some sort of stream nearby. I glanced at her hesitantly; she made a good point, but I didn't normally trust women's opinions. They always led to trouble. My father always used to say, "Best-case scenario for following a woman's suggestion is one year of getting screwed over."

What would he think of me if I were to follow that woman? In addition, the tunnel was safer: it only contained nonpoisonous snakes. Who knew what we would encounter if we walked in the woods? A tiger, a bear, a disfigured ghost? She argued again and I agreed, but we were going to do things my way. We were going to open the tunnel door together and stick a piece of wood in its opening so it wouldn't shut again. We were not going to trek for more than fifty meters in one direction, then we would return to our door and take a different route.

We started to walk. The trees were interspersed with smaller shrubs with tomato-like red fruit. She reached out to grab one, but I warned her, "Do you even know what this is? It could poison you."

She looked at me imploringly, then left it. We walked over fifty meters but didn't find a water source, so we returned. We then wandered along a different pathway that included tall trees, with branches reaching all the way to their very top. Animals that resembled little monkeys sat on the limbs, curiously glancing at us. Thirty meters on, the tall trees disappeared and only smaller ones were visible, with new tall trees showing behind them a long distance away.

We finally encountered a stream of water that cut across our path. Instantly and recklessly, we went to drink from it using our hands, too thirsty to consider anything else. Luckily it tasted like fresh water with a slight tint of bitterness, as though someone poured a little bit of vinegar in it.

We quenched our thirst, but she wished we had a bottle or canteen with us to fill instead of going to the stream every time we got thirsty. We were silently heading back to the tunnel when I asked her about her name.

She answered, without looking at me, "Shadia. And yours?"

"It's Omar."

Learning her name was strange. It was an older name, from the generation before ours. I wanted to ask her why she was named Shadia, but I thought it was trivial question so I asked her what she did instead. She responded while we walked back to the tunnel door, "I'm a government employee."

I asked her teasingly, "Are you one of those employees who tell people, 'Come again tomorrow?'"[2]

She gave me a sharp look—one that you only see coming from an uptight civil servant forced to deal with an annoying citizen who insisted she hurry with his papers before she had even got a chance to have breakfast.

---

[2] A famous Egyptian phrase, widely used by government employees or civil servants to indicate delaying the affairs of customers.

Instead of carrying on with our introductions, she suddenly asked if I was aware that the sun was setting. I noticed from the moment I woke up that day that the sky was yellowish in color, like a windy day, but without sand. I looked up after she made that remark and saw that the sky was orange by then, with a brownish tint to it...

It was the color of Manal Ali's hair—a girl in my high school who was followed by everyone the minute she left school until she arrived at her house, but no one dared open his mouth with her. She once talked to me after a private lesson, but I made a lame response, to which she gave a disgusted look and left.

When we reached the tunnel, Shadia went down first and I followed. It was darker than last time. She insisted we search for a light source, so I told her that it was luminous earlier, in the middle of the day, because of tiny holes in the ceiling. We didn't spend much time discussing it before we eventually looked for a light switch or something of the sort.

We searched for a long time but found nothing. We then sat down in dejection and she burst into tears. I tried to console her verbally, then attempted to pat her on the shoulder but she flinched, so I apologized.

She said, "Even though we're in an exceptional situation, that doesn't mean I'm letting go of my morals." Then she looked away. "I'm sorry. I just never expected to be in the company of a strange man by myself."

I leaned back in disbelief and asked her sharply, "Did you expect to wake up and find yourself in the woods, being chased by large rats?" My words seemed to remind her of the oddness of our situation, which led her to burst into tears once more, so I again apologized, even though I don't tend to do that a lot.

"I'm starving!" she said. But before she finished her sentence, dim lights gradually began penetrating the tunnel. The first thing my gaze landed on was my beloved snake, so I told her it was our only answer for food, but she didn't accept that. She took a fruit out of her pocket, mentioning that she picked it up on her way and assuring me that she saw the little monkeys eating them. I admired her attention to detail; maybe I hadn't done the same thing because I was hoping I could eat my snake.

She split her fruit into two halves. It was similar to a large-sized apple, but contained many small seeds and very little juice. I gratefully said no to her offer—not out of generosity, but because I found the snake to be the safer choice. I started to get on with it while observing her reaction from tasting the fruit. She said it tasted bad, like rotten spinach, but proceeded to eat it anyway. For her, that was still better than eating a raw snake.

Impatient, she said, "I need to go to sleep, please."

What do I have to do with her sleep? She doesn't want me to rock her back and forth or tell her a bedtime story, does she?

"Please, go ahead," I said jokingly, as if inviting her to make herself at home. She asked me to move to an appropriate distance away so she would be comfortable sleeping...far enough away that I couldn't see her. I exhaled irritably. *Does she think she owns the place?*

I left her and explored more of the tunnel. It was becoming more luminous than it was earlier, and its walls were starting to look more damp. After passing the second door—the one from which I went up to her—the tunnel started to take a right curve. My curiosity told me to carry on, so I followed the path and was surprised to notice some light at the end of it: a white light, different from the pale one coming in through the ceiling. I thought it must have some answer to our situation.

"Mrs. Shadia!" I yelled while walking back toward her. My voice echoed in the tunnel and she angrily responded by asking what I wanted, and warning me not to ever use the title "Mrs." before her name again. I told her to get up and come, once again ignoring what she said. She walked behind me until we reached the source of the white light.

The tunnel was blocked with a wall. A large metallic door rose from the ground all the way up to the ceiling. Almost one third of the door exhibited a white light ring. To the door's right, a big flat-screen occupied the rest of the wall. We exchanged confused looks before I tried to open the door, but it was fixed and unmoving. I knocked and it produced a solid sound.

Shadia was inspecting the screen when she suddenly pointed to a small blue button next to the screen with the words PRESS HERE. Without thinking or consulting with her, I immediately pressed it.

She opened her mouth to object, but she swallowed her tongue when the screen lit up in a turquoise color and eerie music came out of it, played with string instruments that I never heard before in my life. The turquoise began to fade out as a strange-looking man appeared on the screen, with a clean white curtain behind him, and he started speaking.

5

He was wide-eyed, with a protruding broad mouth and a big, flat nose. His forehead was large and slanted, and he spoke in a formal voice, similar to that of lecturers, with eloquent Arabic pronunciation.

"Dear Omar, dear Shadia! Welcome to the fourth island of the crescent archipelago. Don't bother trying to recall how you arrived here, as you were drugged when it happened. And don't attempt to interpret or comprehend the purpose of your presence here. I only want you to pay attention to what I say.

"The door next to this screen gives you access to a fully equipped shelter with up-to-date tools and supplies that can last you for years and years. If you choose to open that door, you will remain inside and you won't be allowed to leave for the next three years. During that time you will be required to write down the smallest details of your life from the moment you were born until today, including all the events, feelings, impressions, and thoughts that you have experienced. At the end of each year, you will turn over a part of your entries. Don't worry about how you're supposed to remember your life in detail, as we have a special drug that will help you do that."

The man displayed little to no facial expressions, especially compared to my anxiously perspiring face or to Shadia's, who was almost in tears.

"At the end of each year, you'll get one part of the door code. After obtaining all three parts, you will finally be able to unlock and open the door, which leads to a portal that will let you leave this place."

The man paused for a few moments, giving us the chance to take in what he told us. There was a broad space between his brows that didn't allow him to furrow them, which would have suited what he was about to say next.

"Any attempt at writing down false entries, or making up unreal events, will result in doubling your time. Any attempt to open the door before your time is up will lead to the death of one of you—"

I cursed at him, protesting against what he just said, while Shadia howled in grief and complaint, but before we could go any further, he continued.

"There's an alternative solution. You can search the island for a way out, and if you succeed in doing that, no one will stop you. We will also provide you with three supply bags to help you survive the first few days of your search."

The man smiled, or so I imagined, before he carried on. "But I have to warn you, the island is vast and wildly dangerous. Surviving animal attacks won't be as challenging as being able to feed yourselves, or protect yourselves from the wild environment."

I felt exasperated; the notion that we were nothing but lab rats increased inside of me, while Shadia was desperately muttering next to me with teary eyes. Couldn't that foolish man find someone else to run his experiments on? Why didn't he bring a fit, athletic man and a biology or computer scientist? Couldn't he get anyone other than a flabby man and a chubby woman, both of whom worked in industries that had nothing to do with any sense of adventure?

The screen went dark briefly and another man, who looked very similar but with larger forearms, appeared. His attire resembled a military uniform.

"You can choose to enter the shelter at any time, starting now and up to two weeks from now. During those two weeks you can explore the island, but if one of you dies, the other will lose the privilege to enter the shelter."

Once again they brought up death as though it was no big deal, as if it were just an ordinary step we were required to accept. They dealt with us like two suicidal folks or two commandos. I couldn't help but grin at the idea of a commando named Shadia who was no taller than a meter and a half and who weighed almost eighty kilos.

"After all the instructions are provided, you will find three bags. The first contains tools such as lighters, ropes, and hammers, in addition to a map of the island and an instruction manual. In the second bag you'll find weapons and knives, and in the third, medications, bandages, and a booklet that explains how to use these things. Good luck to both of you!"

The screen went off and a lantern on the ceiling lit up the place. An opening in the wall to our left spotlighted the three large bags. Neither one of us moved—we were in shock as we exchanged glances.

I wanted to do anything but submit to that useless game. Who was running it, anyway? Was it a state intelligence unit carrying out an experiment that tested the strength of humans, or was it a gang of millionaires who wanted to have some fun, or a bunch of irrational people?

Tears silently slid down Shadia's face. I tried to calm her down for what seemed like the tenth time that day, but she fell to the floor and passed out. I inspected her carefully and found that she was breathing regularly, so I decided to let her be and gather my own thoughts. I remembered what the man said about one of the bags containing bandages, so I searched until I found an antiseptic to clean my wounds. I didn't bother covering them with a bandage so our supplies wouldn't run out quickly, especially since the wound was long but shallow. I didn't have the power to search the rest of the bags— I was exhausted and needed to get some sleep. I laid on the ground and surrendered to deep slumber.

In a dream I saw my older sister's husband, in whose house I lived for four years during high school. The jerk was good at undermining me and speaking to me in a manner that boiled my blood, but I could never exactly put my finger on why it did. I was chasing him in my dream. He carried a bag, similar to the one with the bandages, and I ran after him until I lost him in an old neighborhood that looked like the streets of Ghorreya, where I lived during my college years. I froze in place until some dirty water was spilled on my head from the balcony above. I looked up and it was my second ex-wife.

I was a bastard to her. She got pregnant in spite of me, so I left her, and two months later she miscarried. The doctor claimed it happened because of her psychological condition. I didn't believe in that nonsense at the time: I was certain that she was lying so she could win me back and get pregnant again, and then I would have to accept it because I wouldn't want to be responsible for killing two of my children. I was too smart for their little trick, so I divorced her and didn't let it get to me. A while later, I realized how unfair I had been to her and decided to never get married again before I thought long and well about it.

Shadia woke me up, scolding me for being in such a deep sleep and behaving as if we were hanging out at our private house. I didn't know which was worse: the experience or the company. That sharp, hot-tempered woman with highly questionable femininity was too much for me. If I was stuck with a sweet, good-looking, compliant young lady, like Nagat from *Souq Al-Asr*,[3] maybe then I would have chosen to spend three years in the shelter without thinking about it. But my bad luck locked me in with Fathiya from *L'an Aeesh fe Gilbab Aby*.[4]

She asked me what we were going to do. She mentioned the possibility of going on a hunger strike, explaining how it would force our kidnappers

---

[3] *Souq Al-Asr:* an Egyptian TV series produced in 2001.

[4] A she-devil, controlling archetypal character in *L'an Aeesh fe Gilbab Aby*, in English "Falling Far from the Tree": an Egyptian TV series produced in 1996.

to release us from of their game. I scoffed at Shadia and told her they thought our deaths were worthless. The owners of the island were either madmen, serial killers, or, best-case scenario, mad scientists who perceived our possible death to be collateral damage, like a pilot who dropped bombs on a house that contained hundreds of people just to kill one enemy.

She said that she couldn't stay on the island for too long because she was responsible for an orphan whom she was raising on her own—the daughter of her sister, who died in a car accident with her husband. She didn't know what was going to happen to the girl, and who would look after her when she was gone. Shadia's mother was elderly and sick and couldn't possibly take care of her. Her older brother could perhaps take her in, but his evil wife wouldn't treat the child kindly: she would make her wish she lived in an orphanage instead.

Shadia wouldn't share her age with me, but I assumed she was in her thirties and that the kid was around ten, having been looked after by Shadia since she was four. Her ex-fiancé didn't like the idea of a youngster living with them after marriage, so she dumped him. Afterward, no one else would agree to the idea. She said she couldn't find someone who was "man enough" to carry the responsibility of a parentless child. If she rated me according to her standards, I wouldn't be considered a man by any means.

No one is going to look for me. That was the first thought that crossed my mind as I listened to her. My store would remain closed for a while, then my assistant would take over. My cousin Sameer would learn about my disappearance and claim his inheritance. My customers would search for a new plumber, my coffeehouse writer friends would think that I was a jerk who traveled to a country in the Gulf without informing them, and the rest of my relatives would think I either passed away or got rich and forgot all about them.

Nothing much would be affected if I stayed here for three years: I would have food and shelter, and I would write my diaries, beginning with my childhood years, when I used to climb trees, swim in the canal, and play football in Shawadfy's playground. I stole corn and fava beans from the fields and grilled them at night up until my high school days, shifting from one job to another, watching movies starring Adel Emam and Nadia El Gendy.[5]

But the poor soul next to me couldn't stay here when there were people waiting for her return. Her life was part of a whole, and mine was missing the whole.

I decided to risk it for her and attempt to search for a way out. I was going to be a "man"—by her standards this time. I didn't think I lacked manhood and I didn't believe I was a bastard—I never abandoned anyone, but I did spend all my life escaping responsibilities and picking the easy answers. I never chose to fight or stand in the way of obstacles. I always searched for the nearest exit, even if it led to

---

[5] Renowned Egyptian actors.

a less-than-average result. I was going to take a risk this time, not for my own sake, but for that woman whose company I couldn't stand.

6

It was a quiet morning. We first headed to the stream to quench our thirst and fill the water containers we were provided with, then we tasted some of the fruit for breakfast. There were many edible fruits on the island. The manual described each one in detail, as it also outlined the inedible ones: some of the latter could make you nauseous or give you diarrhea, while others might make you hallucinate. Some bad fruits looked extremely similar to the edible fruits. I thought it wouldn't be too bad if I ate some of those at that point. Perhaps I could have used some hallucinations at that time.

Armed with a large knife and an electric cattle prod, I walked with attentiveness and caution. I planned to electrify the first wolf that came my way, then it could tell its pack we weren't an easy target and they would stop chasing us. The area surrounding the stream was packed with fruity shrubs, but the berries were hard to snatch from the branches. I used my knife to cut them out of the bush.

I collected a reasonable amount of fruit to bring back to Shadia, and then we sat together on the ground to pick out the good ones. We resembled two lovers spending time by a river park, even though our clothes were filthy and we both frowned and didn't utter a word.

I tried four different kinds of supposedly edible fruit, but they all tasted unbearable. I stopped eating and cursed a blue streak, finally realizing the value of basic foodstuffs like taro. Shadia, on the other hand, finished eating her fruit and made her plan clear: two fruits rich in energy, one protein concentrated, and others rich in vitamins and minerals. She held on to the booklet and went over each one of them. She frowned a little after the first bite, then swallowed with an effort and carried on.

I suggested we get into the water and bathe with our clothes on, then sit in the sun to dry.

"Don't you ever think?" Offended, I looked at her and she continued, "We have no idea what we might encounter in that water."

I objected, pointing out the stream was shallow and nothing seemed suspicious about it. I got in the water at her challenge, laid my body on its surface, closed my eyes, and let myself enjoy the refreshing feeling in that dry summer weather. For a second, I forgot where I was, imagining myself in an Asian country on vacation. I triumphantly looked at her. She looked away, but she smiled in victory when I started screaming moments later and ran out of the water in fear.

Three black worms were stuck on my face and limbs, pinching me. She claimed they were called "leeches" and that they sucked your blood, which freaked me out even more.

Getting them off was incredibly painful, as each one wouldn't let go without leaving a lesion. She helped me get them off, laughing for the first time. On our way back to the tunnel, I sanitized my wounds, then gave in and ate five fruits. Strangely enough, they managed to fill me up.

One of the bags contained a detailed map of the island, which was semirectangular, even though its western side was rather convex. Its length was seven kilometers at the maximum and its width was four kilometers. To my surprise, there was a small mountain in the west portion of the forest that we hadn't noticed before because of the thickness and height of the trees. The mountain included a waterfall that flowed into a river, from which several streams formed.

Woods stretched to the east and south and were only separated from the shore by few meters. To the north, the river divided the forest, then curved to discharge into a sea at the northern shore of the island, which was separated from the forest by a broad flatland.

"There must be a boat hidden somewhere on the island shore. Do you think that would be the best chance of escape?" I asked her while still looking at the map. She agreed with me, so I began to explain my plan to her: The tunnel was going to be our camp and the river our main landmark. Trekking from the tunnel toward the river, we would hike parallel to the river until we reached the mountain, crossing the river at its source, then walk on the hillside down to the shore.

"We'll travel along the shore starting from where the mountain is, right here," I told her, pointing to the map, "and all the way to the end of the river."

I pretended I was the camp leader in Siwa who explained our roles to my military battalion. My plan meant that we would be done exploring the shore in six days maximum, considering that we would return to our tunnel refuge every evening.

She shook her head in uncertainty, as though she didn't think that whoever brought us to the island would make it that easy. She pointed at the tiny blue dots that were spread on the hillside on the map.

"Can you explain what these are?"

I scratched my head, taking it in. Up until that point, I thought they were just dots that completed the shape, especially since the map was drawn in an artistic manner, not in plain lines. I told her she was overthinking and assuming the worst. She argued with me for a while, but to no avail. At the end of the day, we were compelled to find a way out of that nightmare by working together.

She suggested we bring our supplies and continue our journey around the shore without returning to the tunnel to save time, but I disapproved of the idea. If mornings on the island were that dangerous, nights were going to be way worse. Our bags held two separate sets of tent supplies and sleeping bags, as if whoever prepared them assumed that we would sleep in the open. That was her additional excuse.

I shook my head firmly in disagreement and mumbled to myself, "Best-case scenario for following a woman's suggestion is one year of getting screwed over."

She raised her eyebrows. "So was it me who suggested you get into the water?"

Our discussion intensified, but before we could end it, the sound of roaring water caught my attention. Her eyes stared behind me in astonishment. I turned to see a flood surging from the other side of the tunnel. It reached us and welled up in no time, the water level quickly increasing until it rose above my knees. Shadia screamed, saying she didn't know how to swim. I climbed the steps that connected to the door and attempted to open it. I cursed out loud when it wouldn't widen more than the size of a fist.

It was obvious that the problem was another part of their sick game. It wouldn't be too surprising either if the wolves from the day before were trained and knew exactly what they were doing, since normal wolves would normally tear a person up in that same situation.

I moved to Shadia and asked her to calm down and look in the bags for anything that resembled a hose or a hollow pipe. She wanted to know why, but in anger I told her there was no time to explain. Strangely enough, she submitted and searched her bags as I ordered. She suggested we break the electric cattle prod, since it harbored a hollow pipe inside, but I refused since we couldn't afford to sacrifice that tool.

The water level rose quickly as we kept on searching. She was getting more anxious, aimlessly stirring the items in the bag. The water came higher until it reached my belly button and her lower chest, while the bags were deluged with water, making it impossible to search more. I asked her to climb the steps and hold on to the door since I knew how to swim.

I decided perhaps I could sacrifice the cattle prod and break it if the water level reached the door, turning it into a pipe from which we could breathe by extending it out of the water. I was certain our captors were going to let things reach an unsafe point, torture us for a few minutes, then everything would go back to normal as if absolutely nothing happened. It was all part of their sickening game.

The water reached my neck while Shadia waited on the steps, and I remembered at that moment how the tent bags came with hollow metal stakes, the type of which you can change size. I dove in the water while she called my name in a shaky voice. I reached out to the bags, pulled two stakes from the tent materials, and swam upward.

My feet couldn't reach the ground, as the water level completely filled the tunnel and began to overflow outward through the tiny door opening. Shadia was in an extreme state of shock. Before water covered our entire faces, I explained to her that it was simply part of the game, that we weren't going to die, and then I trained her to breathe through the pipe. We proceeded to patiently and regularly breathe together before she randomly panicked again. I reached out to her, putting my hand on her shoulder, which seemed to calm her down. She went back to breathing normally again.

I couldn't calculate exactly how much time passed, but it was long enough for me to begin feeling extreme exhaustion in my limbs. I held on to the ladder to rest my body, trying as much as I could not to touch her. She began to totter and it seemed that she was about to lose her balance. I reached out my arm to help her collect herself, but her weight relaxed on my arm. Sensing she was ready to let herself fall, I pinched her aggressively. She pushed me away when I did that, but at least it brought her back to her senses. She readjusted her body and grabbed on to the ladder tightly again. Her eyes were closed the entire time, so it was only possible to communicate with her through touching.

After a while, she ran out of strength again. I pinched her, but to no avail that time, and she began to let herself drown. There was no other way to stop it but to hold her myself and raise her body above the water level. At the same moment, the water finally stopped gushing. Its level dropped until it reached the surface of the tunnel, then it stopped altogether.

I put my arm around her and supported her body so her head stayed above water as her eyes remained closed. I shook her harshly and pinched her back with the tips of my fingers until she finally opened her eyes and gasped, attempting to catch her breath. To my surprise, she then rested her head on my shoulder while she continued half-conscious.

I screamed furiously, telling "them" to stop and empty the tunnel's water. I cursed and challenged them to come and confront me if they possessed one real man among them. There was no response. I remained floating in the water, resting with one hand and foot on the ladder. My other arm held on to a half-conscious woman while time passed.

7

The saline solution bag emptied its components through the center opening, landing on the dry gauze that covered Omar's wounds. The bandage absorbed some of the solution, whereas most of it ended up on the floor, taking what was left from crusts and blood along with it. Omar was fearfully waiting for the moment they tried to take off the gauze, and was begging the nurse to take all the time she needed and pour more solution.

He had faced death many times, but in that moment, he was indeed dying, as his heart dropped with every piece of gauze being removed. Sweat exuded from his body in the same amount that blood oozed from his wounds. He was the only patient in the hospital who didn't have a relative with him, but other patients' relatives split shifts to look after him, taking him in like a family member. For instance, an unknown lady accompanied him or held his hands during the wound dressing. Another fed him when needed, a gentleman donated his blood to him, and an elderly woman sat with him at night and recounted stories from the good old days.

He was first found passed out on the ground. The doctors, policemen, prosecutor, and several others asked him how he attained his burns, but he denied knowing. No matter how many times he swore he didn't know, no one would believe him. After he managed to survive the severe sepsis from the previous week, he decided to write down his story as a novel. He had previously tried to compose several short stories and one novel, none of which were read much except by some of his acquaintances.

Dr. Hend encouraged him, telling him that writing would be beneficial for his mental state. She laughed at him whenever he swore that the story of the novel truly did happen to him, and when he insisted that it be stated on the cover that it was based on true events. When he told Dr. Sameh, his other doctor, about it, he urged him to record it as well. Sameh was a dedicated and caring doctor, but he turned into a monster in the dressing room. He didn't care much for Omar's shrieking or whimpering, and he insisted on cleaning the wounds with thorough care, no matter how much it led to horrendous pain. He brutally manhandled the joints, tearing off the dead tissue with the excuse that Omar would otherwise heal in a disfigured manner.

The worst part was when Sameh insisted he sit in a bath when he was extremely feverish. Omar used to previously fantasize about spending time in one of the whirlpool baths he'd seen in some of the fancier houses and villas; he once actually did sit in one when he was supposed to fix some extension cords for a rich client who left him alone in the villa. He filled up the hot tub, sat down in it, and enjoyed the flow of water tickling his body. Now, however, the hospital's whirlpool had become a torture that the doctor claimed was beneficial.

Sameh sat with Omar one night and said that he put him through physical pain for medical reasons, and that too much tenderness on his part would do more harm than good. Omar didn't believe him. He was certain that somewhere on the other end of the world, they would have more sympathy for their patients' pain and would figure out different methods to cure them without putting them through that dreadful agony.

One day, Omar was sitting in his wheelchair with Dr. Sameh in his office. He visited occasionally to drink coffee and for a change of scenery, and Sameh told him he would write for him on that day instead of Ehab, who was preoccupied with a different job and didn't show up. He opened the laptop and started typing Omar's words. Outside the door, four other people eavesdropped on Omar's story.

***

The water level slowly declined and Shadia finally gained consciousness. Luckily she was still exhausted, so she didn't smack my face for physically holding her. I tried once more to push the door, and as I expected, now it easily opened since that part of the game was over for them. I felt like Super Mario in a game designed by a psychotic madman who sat surrounded by ten computers in some rotten basement.

I helped her get up and we sat on the ground, trying to catch our breath, until the tunnel emptied entirely. Shadia was trembling like a leaf. I looked at her and started laughing, so she pouted her lips and demanded to know what was so amusing. I didn't answer her and carried on laughing. It was contagious, so she started to chuckle along with me.

She asked me again, so I said, "If only I had waited long enough, I could have washed myself without getting into that stream and getting pinched by those leeches."

"You always miscalculate things. Just let me take the lead," she answered with a big smile.

She was demanding to take charge, but only few seconds ago, she appeared utterly helpless. Without me, she probably would have drowned at the bottom of the tunnel. I wouldn't have been surprised if she called me "useless," or insisted that I didn't help her.

A while later, I went down to the tunnel to see if there was any water remaining. Of course, to make things worse, the tunnel was now like a shallow lagoon, with water reaching my knees. Those madmen were forcing us to spend the night outside the tunnel. *How stupid I was earlier to feel grateful that they provided tents and sleeping bags!* I didn't realize it was part of their sick idea.

When Shadia found out, she didn't panic as she usually did, but she did curse them. "I won't surrender to their plan anymore. I will sit right here without moving, and I will stop eating until they know that their game has failed. They aren't going to turn us into dolls that they move around whenever they want to."

It was an exciting speech, but only for a different time and place...when you knew who caged you and when your life actually presented any value to them.

I stated firmly, "Right now, we have been kidnapped. No one knows anything about our whereabouts, and no one will know if we both die. There won't be a body, a medical examiner, or a detective inspector to catch the murderers. We're like slaves taken from Africa to work in the New World—we have no choice but to surrender and adjust."

I had never seen trees like these before, not in a TV show or in pictures on the internet. Those animals never turned up in front of me on *National Geographic*. We were on a remote island in an undiscovered ocean—there was absolutely no escape.

She finally agreed. We dragged our bags out of the tunnel one right after the other. She asked me to sit down for a while, as she still felt exhausted and unable to walk a long distance. We got the tent out of the bags, and as soon as we laid it on the ground, her gaze suddenly fixed on something behind me. A group of birds that looked like a hybrid of ducks and geese confidently strutted around and didn't pay us any attention. I didn't think for long before I grabbed the cattle prod and struck one with it, which knocked it down while the others scattered. I chased them and was able to shock another one before the rest all vanished.

I took my knife out and slaughtered them while Shadia stared at me in shock, insisting that she would never eat raw meat. I told her we were going to grill them, since we possessed a lighter and the place was full of dry branches. I started removing their feathers in excitement and told her to gather some wood, but she didn't listen and said, in English instead of Arabic, "Help yourself."

I didn't care much and carried on with my mission, intending to make her beg before I gave her a taste of meat. I finished my task and got up to gather some firewood, but immediately stopped when I saw something coming: a group of felines that looked exactly like the stray cats that filled the dumpsters of our streets. I shooed them, but they didn't step back and proceeded to approach my birds. I was able to save one, but the second ended up fought over by three cats, aggressively meowing at each other as the fight got more intense. They surrounded me, trying to snatch the other bird from my hand while Shadia screamed and dashed off to the tunnel…as expected.

I ran toward the prod and struck one of them, making it writhe on the ground as the rest dispersed, except the three that were fighting over the bird. I approached them confidently and struck one, which let go and rolled around in pain. The second one ran off. As for the third, it stayed still, its jaw holding onto the bird. The prod made another sound, and before I could strike the cat, it released the bird and ran off.

I put the first bird down and seized the other one, checking the bite marks. I assumed that fire would be enough to disinfect their filthy slobber. I thought about giving Shadia the cat-bitten remains if she asked me for a piece, as a way of punishing her.

While I was busy with my triumph, one of the cats deviously sneaked in without a sound and stole the first one from my hand. I ran after it with the electric prod, but couldn't catch it, and when I went back, the second bird had disappeared as well.

I expected Shadia to gloat over what happened, but it was quite the opposite. She consoled me and even brought me some of the fruit that she stored. We settled on having lunch, then moving. I told her that the cat incident reminded me of *The Old Man and the Sea* and explained why the story gained wide popularity despite it being centered around a conflict between an old man and sharks. I then understood its meaning, and how much it affected me. Shadia stared confusedly at me. Apparently she didn't know who Hemingway was in the first place, so how was she supposed to know what *The Old Man and the Sea* was?

We walked for an hour, dragging our bags along: three large packs attached to wheels, with metallic handles. They sometimes got stuck in the mud, so I pulled them out aggressively and we carried on with our hike. We trudged toward the stream, Shadia stopping occasionally to pick up different fruits, seemingly shopping in a vegetable and fruit market.

We reached the steam, drank, and continued to walk alongside it to reach the river. On our way, I glimpsed colorful birds and listened to their warbling. We saw flowery shrubs and rabbit-like animals hopping around here and there. The weather was uplifting and the walk was tranquil, with no wolves or wild animals. I told myself that it must be the calm before the storm.

The mountain appeared for the first time. It was tremendously distant, not possibly closer than ten kilometers. Shadia put down the bags, sat on the ground, got out the booklet, and checked the map.

"The map uses different units to measure distance. It's going to take a much longer time to explore the beaches."

I pointed out that the shore was visible. "We don't have to walk on every inch of it to explore it," I said. She shrugged her shoulders, unconvinced.

We continued walking until the soft sun disappeared and it started to get dark, and decided to camp next to the stream, even though our destination was nearby. We set our two tents and lit a fire between them. Sleeping in shifts was agreed on, since it wasn't safe for us to be asleep at the same time. Who knew what could be waiting?

She asked to sleep first. I agreed and stayed awake, killing time by grilling some of the fruit to discover the effect on their taste. I picked a potato-like fruit and grilled it a little. Before I took my first bite, Shadia's voice grabbed my attention.

"Look at the moon, Mr. Omar!"

I sneered at her and said it was too early for that kind of romance. She angrily responded, "Even a mad person wouldn't peek at you twice. Just look up!"

I was tongue-tied at her coarseness, but I gazed up at the sky and exclaimed, "Oh God!"

8

I was too speechless to get back at that spiteful woman who kept calling me names. Up in the sky were two moons: one in the center, curved as if it was the seventh day of the Hijri month. The second was a small crescent toward the west, near the direction of the mountain. The first thing that crossed my mind was that it was some sort of trick from whoever was in charge.

I felt like I was being punished by God, and if He was punishing me for ten sins, at least seven of the punishments were being carried out through Shadia. The woman went into a frenzy, swearing that we had been abducted to another planet and that aliens were conducting experiments on us.

I seized this chance to scold her rudely, calling her mad, naïve, and ignorant. I was prepared to call her more names if she replied in her usual manner, but she burst into tears instead, so my tone altered completely. She was just a simple woman, bluntly defending herself with a false pretense of confidence and unrealistic independence.

Women are fragile creatures, and they need men's support to set things straight, I said to myself. I knew if I said that out loud, she would have lost it and probably called me ignorant, sexist, and other useless terms.

All I wanted at the time was to go to sleep and leave everything else for the next day. I was willing to let her have her fair share of sleep so she would return the favor, but that seemed nearly impossible. I took a deep breath and tried to persuade her: no other place in the world reported that cat species except Egypt.

She claimed that they could have kidnapped the cats the way they did us, and that everything in that place was bizarre, no matter how similar it looked to things we knew. Every animal was endowed with something different from an Earth animal. No snakes had feet on their torsos; no trees grew with bluish leaves. "Open your eyes and accept what you are refusing to see!"

I told her I was addicted to watching *National Geographic* and *Planet Earth* on the BBC, and I had probably seen stranger things than what she claimed were indicators of a different planet. Yellow and red leaves exist, and odd-looking animals live in remote regions. We weren't plant or animal scientists to categorize and confirm those animals were the myths she was claiming.

She gradually began to settle down and realize it was all part of their game, that all the nonsense we watch in science fiction movies cannot be applied to real life. I begged her to sleep for a little while so I would get my chance to sleep as well, but she told me that she was going to stay awake for the first shift since she'd lost her desire to go to sleep.

I woke up to the light of morning, feeling thankful that Shadia let me sleep for a long period of time. Soon enough the gratitude was replaced with rage when I saw her sleeping on the ground like a rice bag. I was going to shout at her, then stopped myself. *She slept on the hard ground outdoors, instead of getting into her sleeping bag inside her tent.* She obviously had fallen asleep from fatigue, especially since she was sleeping less than a meter away from me.

I let her continue to sleep and got up to explore the place, with the cattle prod in my hand and a sharp knife in my belt. I thought about hunting an animal, and after some miserable trials, I was able to kill a small, plump, slow creature. Its skin was thick and tough, covered with armor. It was hard work to skin it, as the outer layer wouldn't crack until I heated my knife to the point of flame, and then opened it with the knife.

Shadia woke up to the smell of barbecue. She joined me in eating without asking questions about the type of animal or how I acquired it. It was okay...nothing too terrible. If we had some spices and onions, it would have tasted somewhat appetizing.

We went back to our hike; Shadia dragged one bag while I hauled along the other two. To my surprise she initiated a pleasant chat, asking me about what I did—I told her my story was too long. I didn't tell her about the different jobs I failed at when I was a student, but I did tell her what I did post-graduation. I worked as a teacher in addition to my plumbing job in the evening, but the school fired me because I tried to force my students to take private classes with me.

I once was tour guide in a sightseeing company but was quickly dismissed because my English was poor, and I couldn't handle dealing with Egyptian visitors. Plumbing was my only forte. I was good at it and customers often recommended me to others.

For some reason, though, most of the time I used materials for my clients that were poorer in quality than what I claimed. They took a look at the box and believed the parts were indeed manufactured in Italy when they were really made in China. Of course, the packaging was printed from Mohamed Aly Street.[6] I made lots of money and opened a workshop: a steady site for what I do and to sell supplies. The "plumber" job title never bothered me much. It was sufficient that it paid for my two marriages and for my failed emigration attempt, and I still had credit in the bank.

I told her I was a writer and a member of a writing community in my hometown, and in another smaller community that met in a café once a week. I told her I wrote many books and spent an appropriate amount of money on one novel that no one read, and the publisher gave me many copies—there were still more than 100 at home. I told her I compared myself to the poet Al Gazzar,[7] who gained more from

---

[6] A famous old Egyptian street that sells different goods, usually at cheaper prices.

[7] Al Gazzar (also known as Abo Al Hussein Ibn Al Gazzar): An Egyptian poet who lived during the time of Mamluks, during the thirteenth century.

butchering because poetry didn't earn him much money. He once wrote:

> How could I not be grateful for butchery for as long as I live?
> And how could I not abandon literature?
> When with butchery, dogs begged me for kindness
> But with poetry, it was the other way around.

I was a plumber-writer who read a lot to overcome loneliness, but I didn't mention that the reason behind this isolation was a fear of intimacy. I didn't get women and they didn't get me, and I was terrified at the idea of having children.

I talked to Shadia a lot so the time would pass quicker, and also because I hadn't spoken about myself to anyone for a long time. I continued my monologue until we finally found the river right in front us. It was narrow—its width didn't exceed twenty meters—and despite that, I didn't think that crossing it would be a problem.

"I wonder if it has any crocodiles in it!" Shadia said, to which I didn't respond. That subject matter was solely in the hands of the gentlemen who were running the experiment, in which we were rats.

I asked if she thought we were alone, or if there were other victims. She shrugged, saying she couldn't know for a fact, but she assumed it was most probably just the two of us. If there was anyone else, we would have met them by then.

We walked by the river's side for a while as the mountain slowly revealed itself. There was nothing new or questionable, just a regular riverbank with grasslands on either side that separated it from forest trees on its north and south. After a long time, we sat down to rest and have lunch, eating fruit and what was left from the grilled meat.

When we almost reached the mountainside, the falls that poured into the riverhead looked fascinating. I secretly wished we were hanging out together in different circumstances. A large cave also appeared east of the falls, no more than twenty or thirty meters away. She asked me to call it a day so we could sleep in that spot.

It was too early to camp, but she insisted. I asked her if it was a sound idea for me to go and explore the cave, since it might be a better refuge than sleeping out in the open, but she pleaded with me not to leave her alone. She was certainly more scared than before, responding sullenly and not reacting to my usual provocations. I didn't bother much with her, assuming she would sleep that night and wake up to her old self.

We sat between the closest two trees to our left, not far away from the riverhead, each leaning against a tree. She began to doze off, her head nodding in exhaustion. I set up her tent and told her to get into it and rest. I let her sleep and went to make my own tent, then walked toward the river, exploring it to see if I could perhaps find fish to hunt with my prod. That was when it began to rain.

It was a flood, as if the sky doors opened all at once, so I ran to the protection of my tent and observed the rain from its opening. Ponds began to form, and I noted that when they increased beyond a certain limit, the water flowed with the river's current, creating a tiny river parallel to it. A few minutes passed, and then I saw the water sweeping away two of our bags as Shadia put the third in her tent. I ran out of my tent and chased after to save them.

I struggled to drag the two bags across the slippery mud as the river level began to rise, scolding myself for not keeping them in my tent as Shadia did with hers. The sound of the waterfall overflowing became so loud that I sensed myself inside it, and it began to look larger, with much stronger currents.

A handle on one bag broke, so I grabbed it from its side, dragging it through the mud with more difficulty. My feet kept slipping, so I would fall and get back up. Shadia came out of her tent and looked at me—I signaled to her to stay where she was. She stood hesitantly, one foot out the door.

Suddenly, another flood cascaded from the mountain, swallowing the riverbank and everything on it and heading at us with all of its strength.

9

If a talented, detail-oriented author were to write about that moment, he might extensively describe the flood: splattered raindrops splashing everywhere, the mud that stuck to the first wave, and the dry branches that were scattered on its surface, spinning in circles. He wouldn't forget to mention the image of an animal or two fighting not to drown.

He would describe how I stood in my place, turning my head left and right to detect a way out, then looking back at Shadia. She appeared frantic and implored me to save her—the flood was approaching her faster than me. The writer would describe her clothes: how they had begun to look so shabby that they resembled the attire of an underprivileged worker at the end of a busy day at work, the headscarf that slid down her head, and her revealed collarbones. They made her appear like a woman at her husband's funeral, one who filled the room with tears, screams, and lamentations.

He might, however, possibly overlook the bags that concerned me at the time. Losing them meant everything was going to change, as it would force us to submit and return to the tunnel, willingly becoming prisoners for three whole years.

The flood swept Shadia away, then took me. I struggled to reach her, but it didn't work. The water eventually settled down and subsided, although the rain was still torrential and the ground was a muddy puddle.

I walked to her, took her hand, and helped her get up. We leaned on each other to trudge into the forest. Suddenly a second surge towered above and crashed, separating our hands, but it did bring me closer to the bags, so I held on to them. The flood settled down again while I still grasped the bags tightly.

Shadia slogged toward me as fast as the mud allowed her to. She grabbed one of the two bags—the one with the regular handle—while I dragged the one with the broken handle.

The mud kept sticking to her shoes, so she took them off and held them in her hand. I suggested that she leave the bag in that spot. I would return to get it after we were safe from those frequent, destructive waves. We walked ten meters into the forest, then I took off my own shoes to walk easily and went to get the last bag.

A third wave took me by surprise, violently sweeping me away and dropping me in the river. I tried to resist the current, but it overtook me and pulled me farther and farther away. The water saturated me and I felt like I was about to drown, but at the very last moment, I seized a shrub growing on the riverbank. My head started to spin and everything was getting darker when I heard Shadia's voice yelling from afar, chiding me for abandoning her and drowning.

I was starting to lose consciousness, my grip on the shrub weakening. I was somewhat beginning to enjoy the numbness, but it seemed like Shadia begrudged my feeling at ease without her. Her constant screaming forced me to gather my strength, grab on to the shrub more firmly, and climb onto the bank. The rain was starting to subside. Shadia didn't stop shrieking my name while I trudged back to her. I walked parallel to the trees so I wouldn't get lost in the forest, but I anticipated having to run into it at any moment if another wave struck.

Shadia appeared from among the trees, sprinting toward me barefoot—fighting the mud—and repeated my name while thanking God I didn't drown. What happened after that was even more inexplicable than being on the island in the first place: she gave me a tight, warm hug while sobbing. She had finally let go of her conservatism and lost the peculiar ability to fully regulate all of her feelings in front of me. She let her basic human nature, which naturally craved warm company, lead the way. Her head rested on my shoulder as she sobbed and muttered words I didn't quite get, while her arms squeezed around me. I patted her back, overwhelmed by the moment, while my whole face was enveloped in water—either rain or tears, but I wasn't sure which.

The rain finally let up. Everything calmed, and only tears slid down my face at that point, as I felt indescribably defeated. I tried to let go of Shadia so I could sit, but she clung to me. I remained frozen for a while, until she eventually let go of me and apologized.

I said to her, "We're going through an unprecedented situation. It's okay if we're not acting like ourselves." I took her by the hand, leaned my back against a large tree, and sat her next to me as the sky gradually became darker. She inched closer as she dozed off. She laid her head on my lap and I let her slumber, giving in to deep sleep myself.

At that moment I didn't feel the intimacy between a man and a woman, but one of a father and his daughter, and I believe she felt the same way as well. That was the first time I ever felt like a father, letting his daughter doze off on his lap—a feeling I had prohibited myself from ever experiencing due to an unjustifiable, perhaps unhealthy reason...

I was nine years younger than my oldest sister, in whose house I used to live during high school. Her first child contacted a fever and we soon learned that it reached his brain, leaving him paralyzed, both physically and mentally. The weight of the responsibility complicated everything in her life. She went back and forth to hospitals every day. She even gave birth to her second daughter on a day that she admitted her son to the hospital. While she stayed for five days in the female ward, I babysat him, sleeping in the men's ward.

Her struggle was never-ending. When she believed that she had experienced her share of suffering, her second daughter was born with a cleft palate and lips. The baby underwent one surgery after the other while her father sold the only piece of land he'd inherited from his own father to complete her treatment. Her issue was of course less complicated than her brother's, but further complications surfaced when she entered school. Her classmates bullied and made fun of her, not only because of her appearance, but because of her nasality and the abnormal way she spoke due to her cleft problem.

My sister's terrifying journey became the motive that stopped me from ever wanting to have kids. I feared bringing a child into the world who would expose me to all that pain and suffering. My fear was amplified when my sister herself got sick, passed away, and left her children and her poor husband to suffer on their own.

I didn't fear responsibility as much as I feared the idea of watching a piece of me suffer. How could I watch my own child ache every day and have no medication to cure them? A father should be a superhero who can kill monsters if they go near his kids, but how could he defeat that monster if it was an incurable disease that caused unending pain?

I never opened up to anyone about that. I wouldn't sound convincing and might come off as paranoid or negligent, choosing to live my life without responsibilities. The truth was that I simply couldn't look in the eye of any youngster in pain. Even more so my own child.

The following morning was cloudless and tranquil. First thing I did was to bring the last bag from the riverbank. After that we didn't move and spent the time sitting cross-legged under the tree. By the time it reached midday, Shadia had gone back to her witty nature and sharp tongue. We tried to mix our meat with some of the fruit to change its flavor, but it didn't work.

What I found strange was that if I cracked a joke that made Shadia laugh and nudged her with my shoulder in jest, she quickly responded with scolding, rebuking, and a tongue-lashing, as if she hadn't slept on my lap the previous night. She never failed to get back at me. I made fun of her shabby clothes, so she quickly remarked on my crooked nose; I asked her how much she weighed and she commented on my paunch. That was how we spent that day, which meant that it passed peacefully and we slept in our tents.

The following day we returned to the mountainside, and I suggested we first explore the cave next to the waterfall. Perhaps we could find a place where we could ditch our bags and roam free from the heavy weight, to which she grudgingly agreed. The opening of the cave was two meters above the ground, and the terrain beneath it looked difficult to climb, except for a small part near the waterfall. Climbing was indeed challenging—we fell a couple of times before we finally reached our goal. Shadia mumbled to herself the whole time about my defective ideas and miscalculations.

We entered the cave and lifted our bags up with a rope, then we took a moment to explore. The cave was broad and long, extending deeply inside the mountain. Its ceiling was covered in thorny stones, its ground was rocky and uneven, and its walls were smooth, as if they'd been evened out by a plasterer, except for some subtle raggedness here and there. The cave went uphill and we didn't know where it ended. We left the bags at the opening and walked around to further explore it.

After roaming for about 100 meters, we realized that it stretched straight ahead and gradually became narrower, with some sort of light toward its end. We walked faster, filled with curiosity to learn what was at its end, ignoring side passages that started to appear.

We reached the end of the cave and spotted a sea. It extended forward, seemingly endless, as if there were no shore nor any other land nearby. I looked up and down and noticed that the mountain formed an upright, level stone ledge—one that looked like it was cut by a knife—and then a narrower stone ledge met with the water. The waves slammed against the rocks, the sky was pale, and the sea looked gray with a tint of yellow—there was nothing blue about it. The rocky shore to our left stretched ahead, but the one on our right side extended only for few meters. This made me assume that the opening was next to the plain bulge we saw on the map. The exterior protuberance was met by the decline that contained the waterfall.

"Is it possible that the boat we've been searching for is anchored on the rocks right here?" Shadia asked, but I didn't respond. At that point, anything was possible. It was conceivable that there wasn't a boat—not even a felucca.[8]

"The man on the screen mentioned an 'archipelago' and that it was the fourth island. So where are the rest of the islands?" I wondered.

She impatiently said, "He also said 'crescent,' which means in the shape of an arch. Maybe this beach is at the back of that arch and the rest of the islands can be seen from another beach."

---

[8] Felucca (in Arabic فلوكة): A traditional small wooden sailing boat.

We suddenly heard a buzzing from an unknown source. A voice said abruptly, "One third of the time you were given to find a way out of the island has passed, and you haven't achieved anything yet. My advice to you is to return the shelter and open the door. What you have seen so far is incomparable to what is in store for you. I wish you good luck in making the right decision."

I froze in place as I heard the words while Shadia screamed aloud, challenging our captors: "Reveal yourself and I will show you what you can't handle!"

She was undoubtedly crazy! What could she possibly gain from all this yelling?

"Are you insane? He's not a fruit seller who just sold you some bad grapes," I scolded. She warned me to never call her insane again, so I mentioned that she didn't speak very respectfully to me either. We both eventually shut up as we walked back to the cave's opening.

I wanted to patch things up, so I asked about her niece. She didn't respond and looked away. I was about to speak harshly to her again, but we heard a crackling sound coming from the opening of the cave. We ran quickly to the sound only to find a metal door—which appeared out of nowhere—lowering slowly and closing the cave. We sprinted to pass underneath it before it closed, but it was already too late.

10

The instructions were clear, but we refused to move forward in their game. Our patience had run out. We'd encountered death several times, and that wicked man just declared that everything we went through was nothing compared to what was about to come. My companion was in a state of shock for the tenth time in less than a week, and I didn't have the means to calm her down. We were terribly entrapped in a way that made the company of wild animals and heavy floods seem like a walk in the park.

She finally began to speak. "I miss my niece! She's really more of a daughter. Even long before my sister's passing, I was like the mother who didn't give birth to her."

She kept talking and it seemed to be an overwhelming kind of love that compensated for her lack of success in romantic relationships. Shadia enjoyed reading romantic novels so much that she fell in love with a man who wrote a couple of silly Facebook posts and called himself a writer. He wrote stuff that supported and defended women—everything that Shadia was missing from men—and he made these things sound like the basic foundation for any relationship. She quickly became invested in him and eventually sent a message, to which he replied. They began to correspond frequently, back and forth, after which he became her whole life: one that she lived between the screen and the keyboard.

I didn't understand what exactly reminded her of all that. What I was certain of was that she didn't continue the rest of her story because the voice interrupted her. It sounded deep, like an old radio presenter's voice who worked in the BBC.[9]

"There is a survival button. If you press it, the door will open for you. You will then, however, be forced to head to the shelter and announce your defeat. The alternative is to search the cave with its passages for twenty small keys, all of which you need to insert in their right locks. After that, you will be required to open them in order for the door to rise."

I cursed the man in exasperation and told Shadia to ignore everything he said and go back to our previous conversation instead. She liked my suggestion.

"They will eventually get bored if we remained seated right here, and they will open the door," she said.

I asked her, "Anyway, how did you find out that the guy was a bastard?" She questioned how I realized that piece of information, so I answered sarcastically, "Because your relationship didn't work out, so he must be the one at fault. Women are naturally angels, of course." She told me that she was going to recount the story and let me judge for myself.

We certainly lost it at that point. We were both completely ignoring the disaster we were involved in

---

[9] BBC: A popular Arabic radio station run by the BBC World Service.

so we could discuss a hopeless love story that wouldn't save us from thirst or hunger.

Her story, in a nutshell, was that the man claimed he loved her so she would let him into her life and tell him specific and personal details, and then he turned them into the material for his first novel. He'd used this cheap trick with other women as well, which she found out by chance. She confronted him about it, but he denied everything. He pretended to be mad at her, then kicked her out of his life with the excuse that mistrust meant that their relationship was over.

I interrupted her epic love story to suggest that we needed to search for a way out of our situation. Maybe a different outlet in another cave, near our opening but also in the direction of the sea.

She frowned irritably. It looked like she was blaming herself for opening up. I said sharply, "As I said, he turned out to be a jerk and the rest is history."

She swiftly stood up, angrily stomping on the ground. "I'm going to look for the keys on my own. You look for a place to escape from, since you're obviously used to escaping like burglars."

I was so tongue-tied at the way she spoke that I didn't respond. It occurred to me that I felt like being stuck in an absurd movie with no known ending.

I turned around and walked back toward the opening of the cave that overlooked the water. If the waves were as calm as we last left it, I could execute my plan and save us from the situation, proving to her that she couldn't do anything without me. Our arguments and bickering were a way of escaping what we were going through, for if we let our brains become completely overwhelmed by the situation, we would go entirely mad, or maybe give in to their plan quickly. If someone gave me the option for this adventure while in the comfort of my house, I would never choose to participate in an undertaking that potentially could end in my death... Even if it meant proving a woman wrong.

Maybe I told myself at some point that I wanted to help her, or that it was my main motive, but my stubbornness and pride were the larger factors. I couldn't bear the idea of being a hamster imprisoned in a cage—quite the opposite of being a lion whose robustness and perseverance were being tested. In both cases, I was an animal partaking in an experiment, but the second scenario didn't hurt my pride. On the contrary, the notion of being challenged was helpful to my many inferiority complexes.

Every time I overcame one of their calculated ordeals, I wanted to look them in the eyes challengingly and tell them, "I am much smarter than you and your sick ideas."

To tell you the truth, I don't know why I refused to enter their prison, or their "shelter": it could be from wanting to challenge them; or fear, self-hatred, or masochism; or maybe all of the above.

I reached the exit that overlooked the sea. I carefully searched the area surrounding it and spotted another nearby opening that was one meter above the water's surface. I hesitated before jumping, wondering if the hole didn't lead to anything but another small cave. Then I would be in trouble, not being able to climb up to the first opening again. I would have to walk on that stone ledge for several kilometers. The waves might even rise and take me in, and there could be sections that didn't even have a ledge to walk on. Then I would have no idea what to do.

Despite that, I followed my guts and carefully went down, walked to the other opening, and climbed into it. It led to a long passage that rose upward gradually. I trekked an unknown distance until I reached a dead end. I didn't know what to do, so I hiked back to the mouth of this cave, returning with nothing at all.

Before I reached the opening, I sat on the ground to rest my feet and think about my next step. As far as I knew, Shadia was lost and didn't know what she was doing either. Maybe she had come to her senses and was searching for me to apologize.

Outside the cave it began to rain, and I assumed it was going to cause high waves, making it impossible for me to walk on the stone ledge. A few minutes passed and I spotted water on the ground—not coming from the rain, but rather a leak inside. I walked back and was surprised to see that the water came from a crack in the wall. I put my hand on it: the walls around it were thin. I punched it, which made part of the wall break down, revealing a side passage.

The tunnel had a break in the ceiling through which rain fell heavily. Light infiltrated the tunnel through that orifice as well.

I temporarily moved past the opening, but I decided to return later to learn if it led to a bigger opening toward the upper part of the mountain, from which I could possibly escape.

I continued striding through the side tunnel, which became darker. I walked hurriedly in hopes of reaching the original cave or Shadia, whom I assumed was dying of fear at the time. I finally reached my destination, gazed at the door, then looked toward the sea's direction, but I didn't find her.

I loudly called her name time after time: "Shadia, where are you? What are you doing?"

Eventually until her voice reached me from afar, sounding like it was coming from one of the side tunnels. "None of your business. Continue searching for an opening and leave me alone," she responded with her usual quickness.

I laughed to myself, thinking, *I missed you, you troublesome woman.*

Some time went by and she still hadn't come, so I yelled out for her, angrily this time. Then she appeared with a look of triumph on her face.

"Eighteen out of twenty keys, and you're still walking in circles!"

I looked at her in disbelief. Apparently I had taken my time earlier, and possibly even fell asleep. I wanted to ask if she was scared when I left her—did she look for me? But I kept those questions to myself because I knew she would make my blood boil.

She sat down to catch her breath and claimed that she felt hungry.

"I could hunt a fish, but we'd have to eat it raw," I suggested. She refused in disgust. Then we got up to search in the rest of the side tunnels, but to no avail. Time passed and we examined the tunnels again, one after the other, feeling the walls and the ground with our hands, but still couldn't find anything. Nighttime arrived and we were drained and starving as the cave became entirely dark.

We eventually gave in to sleep. After we woke up, our overpowering feelings included only hunger and thirst. We went to the tunnel with the dead end in hopes of finding some leftover rain. We successfully discovered some running water at the bottom of the wall.

It occurred to me to climb upward to the break in the tunnel's ceiling; perhaps it would lead to the top of the mountain. From there we could possibly walk until we found a spot from which we could safely climb down. Shadia refused my proposal and suggested that we search again.

"Maybe we neglected a spot here or there. Just let me explore by myself. It seems like you jinxed my search process when you joined me."

I didn't argue or remind her that the game was designed that way: it gave you false hope and then became more difficult when you got close to winning.

A whole day passed without achieving or finding anything: she searched, I searched after her, and we repeated the search. A little before nighttime I said, "I am going to climb up to the ceiling break in the tunnel, and so be it."

"It will get dark soon; we can wait until morning to see better."

"I am too anxious to wait a whole night."

She agreed but insisted on coming along, since the tunnel was narrow and scaling it would be easy. We agreed that she would go first, under the condition that I was allowed to physically save her if she lost her balance and fell.

Climbing was indeed easy, but the top was quite far away. We finally reached it in a worn-out state. It was, however, worth the exhaustion. Not because we found an exit, but because the view from the top of that mountain erased, for a few moments, the disaster we were enduring.

11

The top of the mountain was bumpy and rocky. Some plants grew within the rock cracks and the headwaters were close to the opening from which we exited. The waterfall challenged the rules of nature: water rushed up between the rocks through hundreds of small openings, bubbling and moving onward, gathering in one current that headed toward the bottom of the mountain.

The view of the skyline was what I found most fascinating. I felt as though I were on a tourist trip to an island I'd only seen in pictures and never dreamed to visit in reality.

The forest from the top view revealed blue-colored leaves intermingling with leafless branches. The river separated them and flowed in a curved course, unlike the one drawn on the map. Other islands appeared from afar, containing both plant-covered mountains and bare, rocky ones like the one we were on.

The sunset was magnificent, as though the sun dove into the water and was not just veiled behind it. Its goldenness took over the water's color; it looked as though part of it was truly underneath the water and the other part was above, leaving the skyline painted with various colors from yellow to magenta.

The two moons rose in the sky with the setting of the sun, visibly shining. I tried to explain to Shadia a phenomenon I'd read about. In certain regions in the North Pole, the sun sometimes appears as three. This island could potentially have a similar phenomenon, but I couldn't explain why one moon looked smaller than the other.

Shortly after, the beauty of the scenery was overtaken by our extreme hunger. We brainstormed about the potential options, and I suggested we could taste some of the plants but she disapproved, claiming that they could be poisonous, or at least extremely bitter. We walked south for a little bit, but the mountain was tremendously steep, making it impossible to descend.

Desperate and famished, we returned to the opening on top. Before we arrived, I asked her to search for a hidden key in the surrounding area between the grass and in the narrow cracks. We explored for a long time until Shadia decided to sit down in exhaustion and asked me to rest for a bit too.

I lay on the ground next to her, shut my eyes for some time, then opened them. I looked at the sky and the two moons, then contemplated Shadia's face. Was she truly average looking, or was her kind of beauty way too common? Her good looks were a pure rural Egyptian type, even though she was from Cairo. You took one look at her and envisioned her trekking back from the fields where she had been walking her livestock, or her hands holding a full milk container from the cow she'd just milked, offering it to you with a generous and welcoming face.

I could never imagine her as a woman sitting behind a desk, grumpily going over paperwork and then asking for more papers and a ten-pound stamp. With a catty smile, such a woman would cunningly hint that a bribe must be paid if anything was to be done. Could she really be that type? Was she a character to say "Come again tomorrow" or one to say, "Have a wonderful day"?

We descended to the first cave and stared at the red button near the opening: "The key to survival," as they called it. Silently considering it, I knew we both were trying to hold on to the tiny hope of escaping our distresses.

I told Shadia, "I'm sorry I didn't listen to you, and that I didn't take your feelings seriously."

"Save your apology. Neither of us has been through this before."

I found myself inquiring about the governorate[10] she was originally from. She said her entire family lineage was from Cairo.

I guessed wrong, then.

We remained quiet for a while, then I asked where she studied. She didn't say anything. I repeated the question, but she responded wearily, seemingly starting to fall asleep. I let her be and attempted to go to sleep myself but couldn't, which forced me to think about our decision again.

---

[10] Local Egyptian government contains five territorial units: 1) governorates 2) regions 3) districts 4) cities 5) villages.

It occurred to me to get up and press the button while she was sleeping. Maybe she subconsciously wanted me to make that decision for her, without letting her know. That would absolve her of any guilt she felt toward leaving her niece.

Do I press it and end that tragedy, or do I not want it to come to an end yet? I asked myself.

I fell asleep and experienced one nightmare after the other, intermixed with some absurd dreams. I woke up to a strong need to empty my bladder. I walked away from Shadia until I reached an appropriate distance. It suddenly crossed my mind on the way back that we hadn't searched in the broken tunnel wall that led to this main cave.

I sprinted toward it in a hurry, and began to carefully dismantle what remained of the rocks. I felt between them—along with the cave wall as well—but to no avail. That time, I sat in complete misery. Finding glimmers of hope, then being defeated repeatedly, was more painful than failing only once.

Now if I actually press that button, I won't feel an ounce of regret. I've tried my best. I can spend three years feeling good about myself—I attempted to solve their puzzles and exposed myself to danger several times.

I accidentally dozed off and woke up to Shadia's voice. I yelled as loud as I could to let her know where I was. I almost began to hallucinate from hunger. I told her to wait until I returned.

I trudged along heavily, with different hallucinations and visions appearing right in front of my eyes. I reached Shadia, who said she'd inserted eighteen of the keys in their right places, and there were only two left.

"It's hopeless! I can't do it anymore," I said.

She looked at me with teary eyes. "Wait until the middle of the day, then do whatever you want."

Time passed slowly as we remained seated and helpless, barely able to get up. She wept silently, and nothing interrupted her tears except for her prayers and some muttering. I wanted to talk to her so the time would pass faster, but I was too drained.

I tried to get up to bring water, but my feet failed me. I gazed furiously at the door, then looked at the survival button—a large round button like usual emergency switches behind glass. It protruded from the wall; I reached out and stuck my hand in the small area between the button and the wall. There were the last two keys! I screamed ecstatically and cursed them out loud.

12

A couple of uneventful days went by; we got up early in the morning, walked for as long as we could, and explored the beach. We camped at night, sleeping at whichever point we reached. Midday we reentered the forest, where I tried to hunt down a meat source and Shadia picked fruit from different trees. From those we attempted to create recipes from the available options. Shadia found a shrub similar to that of peppercorn. Inside its fruit were seeds with a smell similar to allspice. When we added these ingredients to the meat I captured, they somewhat improved its taste.

Those four days reminded me of camping trips. Most of the time we forgot what we were going through and simply enjoyed ourselves. We even swam in the sea once at some point, like vacationers.

On the fifth day, we reached the river's source, forcing me to confront a question I'd delayed answering: How were we going to cross the river to continue exploring the island? It wasn't that vast—I could swim across it, but Shadia couldn't swim. And what about the bags we dragged along?

We considered choosing a small tree to cut down, then cross the water together while leaning on the sapling. We eventually picked one, camped next to it, and began attempting to cut it down. It wasn't an easy task: our small axe wasn't that strong.

When Shadia saw me put the axe down in frustration, she grabbed it to continue.

"Patience is a virtue, and we still have some time anyway. If we continue trying to knock the tree down, I'm sure it will eventually happen, even if it takes a day or two."

Day after day, her true colors were being revealed. She was kind and well-intentioned, and her emotional walls—which made her appear sharp-tongued and repulsive—were beginning to crumble. From time to time she still spoke bitter judgments and talked back to me challengingly, but she really possessed a sweet nature.

She was occupied with cutting the tree down while I watched her, smiling. Abruptly we saw a man hastily running toward us. He looked like the people from the screen videos—short and broad shouldered, with wide eyes that had a large space between them, and the same slanted forehead. I asked myself, *Are they brothers, or do they all belong to the same family? A mad family that kidnaps people and practices sick games on them!*

He spoke in classical Arabic. "I have finally found you two!"

I wonder why they all use that dialect?

He reached out his hand. In response, I made a fist and aggressively punched his jaw. He was taken aback, as it knocked him down to the ground.

"I just want to help!" he said.

I didn't believe him, assuming it was part of the game. I attacked him again, but he was too strong. He threw me, so I fell on my head and got back up, but he knocked me down and immobilized me with his powerful arms.

Shadia approached, trying to intervene, so he yelled at her, "Just wait! Listen first, then do whatever you want!"

The man explained that we had indeed been kidnapped. He said it in a way that indicated it was a strictly confidential secret. Shadia told him off sharply, saying that it didn't require much intelligence to figure that out.

He clarified. "I mean permanently kidnapped to this planet."

My heart sank in my chest. "What planet are you talking about?" I skeptically asked.

"Planet Editia."

Shadia let out a frantic scream. I cursed him, accusing him of lying and claiming that he was just another part of the game. What he said didn't make any sense, and he looked like the two men in the video.

He said, "The two of you appear similar. We are entirely different from the humans who exist on planet Earth. Think of it—you frequently think all the people in another race look alike."

Then he asked us to follow him carefully to a quieter place, away from all the traps, so he could get a chance to talk.

"My name is Baldreek. The island contains sensors that detect anyone from our race, and they activate weapons to attack because this island is specifically designed to experiment on Earthlings. Editians aren't allowed to be here."

Shadia and I, in one voice, refused to follow him, but he insisted it was for our own good. Baldreek said he was part of an opposition group that protested experimentation on Earthlings, and that he was putting his own life in danger to help us. We still didn't believe him: everything he said sounded like gibberish from a mad person.

"Okay, then," he said. "I will recount the entire story from the start. But promise to join me if the sensors begin to attack at any point."

I sarcastically promised him to do it, eager to hear what he said.

"You are part of a program designed to select the most superior male Earthlings and use them to solve a bigger issue that is common among our newborns—"

Shadia raised her eyebrows in astonishment. "Then why would they bring me if they want to select males?"

Before Baldreek could answer, we heard a buzzing. He got up, flinching, and said, "The sensors have found me... Please follow me!"

That time we ran and followed him. I'm not sure why... Perhaps because there was no other option.

He dashed between the trees in a zigzag pattern as we panted behind him. A group of harpoons were suddenly shot at him from the direction of the trees, which he managed to avoid with an excellent jump. They were small harpoons, hardly longer than twenty centimeters, but were apparently able to end Baldreek's life if aimed at the right spot.

He continued to run, but Shadia and I stood still in fear, so he stopped. We began to move away from Baldreek; he came back and beseeched us to follow him. Reassuringly, he explained that those weapons wouldn't harm Earthlings—only Editians. We hesitated for a moment until another group of harpoons were released. He avoided most of them, except for one that pierced his leg.

Baldreek cried out in pain and pleaded with us to follow him, saying that we were getting close to a safe spot. We remained tentative, not knowing what to do.

"Nothing matters anymore. Being on a different planet means I am already dead," Shadia said.

I scolded her, insisting he was lying and sure that he was only trying to make the game more exciting for our captors. The notion of being on a different planet was practically unthinkable.

After a fairly long debate between us—accompanied by Baldreek's constant begging—we eventually decided to follow him. He limped forward as many more harpoons were discharged, but again he managed to avoid them all except one that scratched his face.

It was crazy: one almost hit me, but it miraculously avoided me. It turned to a different direction right before touching me. It seemed that at least part of what Baldreek said was true.

***

Sitting in his wheelchair in the corridor that separated the intensive care unit from the regular hospital rooms, Omar watched two sick children frolicking together and smiled. One of them sat in a wheelchair while the other pushed it along the corridor, then they exchanged roles. They were playing and enjoying themselves as if they were both healthy and not experiencing tremendous daily pain in the wound dressing room, or receiving their medication in shots all day long, or having blood withdrawn for tests. That was the first time that Omar smiled in the past three days...since the death of the patient who shared his room.

At the time he felt as though he was at death's door; it was only a matter of days before doctors rushed to his room and carried out unsuccessful cardiac resuscitation in an attempt to bring him back to life. The doctor reassured him, telling him his roommate didn't die from the severity of her burns, but from a blood clot that formed in her leg and then moved up to her lung. Omar didn't believe him. She wasn't his first roommate to pass away. The very first one also did, and they claimed his burns were more critical. The second one supposedly inhaled too much smoke. Each roommate stayed with him for a period of time, then went to meet their Creator, and he was realizing that it was his turn now.

One of the kids asked, "Who's faster, Mr. Omar? Me or him?" Omar smiled and requested that they go again so he could judge more accurately. One of the kids' mothers yelled at them and scolded them for playing, so they pouted and went back to their rooms.

The mother approached Omar and asked him why he looked grumpy. "Because of you!" he responded. "You interrupted their happiness, and my short-term delight, too."

"You haven't been yourself since earlier this morning. Something is different. I am sure your case isn't as severe as you think, and don't forget that we're all waiting for you to finish your story."

He asked her to help him get back to bed, and when she got him there, he asked her to open his phone and call a number.

A man picked up the phone and a voice warmly responded, "I'm sorry, I still haven't reached out to my relative to ask him about your cousin's case. I'll get back to you as soon as I possibly can."

Two days after Sabah's passing, Omar called that man—a friend of his and a relative of a famous plastic surgeon. He explained that his cousin had suffered burns over 60 percent of his body, and asked about the probability of his death. He didn't mention that he was the patient. He thought that way the man wouldn't hide the news if it was terrible.

Om Mariam, another patient, entered the room and informed the woman that her son was misbehaving in his room and wouldn't go to sleep, so the mother left the room, muttering threats. Om Mariam took over the task of helping Omar settle in his bed. She was ready to leave the hospital—her wounds were healed almost completely—but promised to visit everyone regularly.

Omar was surprised when she later asked his opinion in an extremely personal matter. Perhaps she perceived him to be between life and death, so he was more likely to give her genuine advice. She told him what she didn't tell the doctors: that she burned herself on purpose. It wasn't the gas burner. She did it because she was living with her daughter in her husband's family's house, and her husband himself lived in a country in the Gulf. Her brother-in-law harassed her, using looks and double-meaning words at first, then with obvious physical advances.

"I informed my husband, but he was furious at me and accused me of lying to create a fallout between him and his brother. He thought I wanted to live independently away from his family. Then my mother-in-law accused me of wanting to move out so I could live indecently."

The accusations hurt her deeply, so she set herself on fire in a moment of desperation, but was able to put it out before things got too bad.

She asked for his opinion: Should she go back to her husband, or should she ask for divorce? She claimed that he'd realized his mistake and promised to buy her a separate house near her own family's house, but she said that a crack had formed between them nonetheless. A friend advised her to get divorced and her mother told her to hang on and have patience. She was lost in between.

"If you love him, you have to forgive," Omar said. "He is living by himself abroad and he's going through a lot of pressure. Being away isn't letting him see the full picture, which clouds his judgment.

The biggest mistake you made was setting yourself on fire, because the rest can always be dealt with."

"I'm not crazy about him, but we're used to one another and share cordiality, like many married couples do," she said.

Omar then asked her to balance the circumstances rationally. She could ask her father to sit with her husband and acquire guarantees that would assure her rights.

She thanked him and prayed that he would be reunited with Shadia soon. He laughed, asking her, "Why would you think we are together?"

"My intuition is always right."

He inhaled, thinking about the whole story, the nature of his feelings, and the next step he should do before his hour came. He felt that was more sooner than later.

13

Fortunately, our journey wasn't too long. We ran on bumpy, tree-lined pathways while being chased by those small harpoons, which were more specifically aimed at the leader of our brief journey—that short, sturdy man with the large face that resembled the faces of the other two men in the video. All their faces looked familiar, like I'd seen them before in some movie or TV show.

Baldreek suddenly stopped and pressed on a tree trunk. A square body, resembling a box but the size of a microbus, emerged. He opened one of its doors and invited us to enter. Cautiously, we got in the box and found ourselves in a narrow room that barely fit three, and sat on small chairs. As soon as we came in, Baldreek opened a bag from which he brought out a tin box and an injection needle. From the tin box he removed a sticky substance and rubbed it on his leg wound, letting out a painful groan as soon as it touched his body. He then stuck the needle in his shoulder and emptied its components out.

"We are safe now, so I can answer all your questions," Baldreek said with the hint of a smile, and began to recount the story.

> It all started around 200,000 years ago, when my ancestors traveled from planet

Earth to this one. Before that, they lived on Earth for more than 100,000 years and cultivated their own society in a region isolated from the rest of humans. Their culture started when nine families settled on a riverbank. They discovered agriculture and had empathy for animals at a time when other people didn't know anything except hunting.

With the passing of time, their way of life developed and spread, and after 100,000 years, they were able to create tools that helped them discover the universe. You have to understand that this was at a time when other human beings were still living as cavemen, feeding on prey or collecting fruit. My ancestors were those whom Earthlings now call "Neanderthals." You believe that branch of humans ceased to exist and were replaced by modern-day humans.

The stories surrounding how our ancestors discovered Editia and were able to travel there differ. Some claim that the results of one experiment led to a universal imbalance that built a connection between Earth and Editia, and that they were able to travel there because of their scientific progress. Religious Editians claim it is a divine command that ordered them to leave Earth after the God of Destruction sabotaged Creation and infected Earth with a disease that was impossible to escape, but they can't agree on what kind of disease led to that godly command.

Baldreek said that last sentence in a way that indicated sarcasm while Shadia whispered to herself, praying for God's grace. I listened to him carefully, still perceiving the whole thing as a trap. I asked him what nonreligious Editians thought about that myth.

He responded that they came up with different theories: the most prominent one was that a natural disaster took place on Earth, like an ice storm or a continental drift. They believed that their ancestors were a lot more technologically enlightened than they currently were, so there must be a scientific reason for their migration. Natural disasters and previous wars on Editia evidently had degraded their development so they in no way were able to maintain their ancestors' level of scientific progress.

"Stop recounting myths and stories—we're not in a history class! All we need to know is why we were kidnapped and brought to this place." I shook my fist and added, "And how do you speak such perfect classical Arabic?"

"The language you hear is a result of a telepathic translator program. You hear the whole conversation in Arabic, but in reality, I'm speaking my own language and I hear you speaking in my language right now."

I twisted my lips in doubt, whereas Shadia opened her mouth in shock for a reason I didn't understand. Baldreek proceeded to narrate the story.

> Around a century ago, the number of male infants decreased drastically. Of

course, different theories have emerged. Some claim the situation is related to the prophecies in holy books that state this was bound to happen, and to them it means we must return to our ancestors' original homeland.

This has concept led to the prominence of religious groups. They have taken over the government, even though nonreligious groups still keep some of their authority and the opposition party remains active and opinionated. The religious groups have concocted the idea of bringing Earthlings here and running experiments on them. They say it's to study your behaviors and reactions to further understand how we can coexist with you after we emigrate.

Shadia finally interrupted him. "How are they planning to do that? And what land are they intending to live on? Our planet is already too occupied as it is!"

"They intend to return to a geographical location similar to the one our ancestors lived in, according to the religious verses," he said. "We have advanced techniques to help them colonize the original land of our progenitors and build borders to separate us from the rest of humanity. As for the people who currently reside there, they will be forced to either choose between staying there under their rules, or leaving."

"But that's unfair!" Shadia said.

"More like a sci-fi movie," I sarcastically added. I didn't believe one word of what he just said, and still clung to my belief that it was part of the game.

Baldreek ignored me and responded to Shadia. "Nonreligious groups are protesting against the idea, saying it is immoral. They suggest running experiments on only a limited number of humans to compensate for our lack of male infants, either by using gene therapy or via mating between male Earthlings and Editian females!"

I was repulsed by the idea, presuming females on Editia would be an eyesore.

"And what kind of genetic disorder are you suffering from?" Shadia asked.

I laughed at her, wondering how she could possibly comprehend an iota of these topics when she was so uncultured. Everything she learned was from Facebook posts, in addition to a couple of cliché romantic novels.

The man mentioned something about a "telomere defect in the Y chromosome." Then he added, "This flaw is present in all males here, but in varying degrees. If mild, it will have no effect. But it can cause death in infancy, sterility, or severe illness. We need males from your planet to bring forth new generations with intact Y chromosomes."

I didn't understand, but Shadia nodded all the way, which I found especially astonishing. She was a government employee who'd never heard of Hemingway or Bahaa Taher,[11] but she knew all

---

[11] Bahaa Taher (in Arabic بهاء طاهر): Renowned Egyptian novelist and short story writer.

about chromosomes? I impatiently asked Baldreek to cut the scientific specifics short and tell us the important details, but Shadia wanted to go over something else.

"So in your story, religious groups are immoral and nonreligious groups aren't?"

He laughed mockingly. "Whoever is in charge is looking for his own good, be it financial or authoritative or religious. For example, one of the leaders in the opposing party aspires to come up with a cure from the experiments on Earthlings—one intended to produce enormous financial gains. Others in nonreligious groups agree with both suggestions and crave the tons of money they can swindle from the emigration to Earth."

That was the only part in his story that made me consider its validity...that he could possibly be telling the truth. Or perhaps Baldreek was one of those who wanted to run experiments on Earthlings but was trying to use emotional manipulation so we would consent.

The room suddenly began to shake, which made me and Shadia panic, but Baldreek reacted calmly and simply pressed some buttons on the wall behind him. The shaking reduced, but then it jolted abruptly, as if it were being slammed against by a heavy body.

When we asked what was going on, Baldreek said, "Apparently the sensors found out where we are and have released an irritating substance to cover the means of transport. It provokes animals, which is why they're attacking it."

"Vehicle? This room is a vehicle?" asked Shadia, to which he nodded.

"It's a self-driving, camouflaged conveyance that can't be seen by the naked eye and doesn't appear on the cameras set up all over the island."

We held on to our many follow-up questions, as we didn't have enough time to ask them. The transport started moving, jolting every once in a while due to the ramming of animals into it, until we reached the riverbank. The vehicle advanced upon the water as Shadia and I remained in shock. It crossed the river, then stopped, while we watched our route through the video screens hung on the wall opposite to the door.

An explosion shook our ride and signs of apprehension began to show on Baldreek's face, but he reassured us that only he was in danger. The explosions were repeated a couple of times, then suddenly stopped. He tried to move the vehicle, but it wouldn't budge. Shortly after, we heard the sound of a metal body ramming into the small door. Seconds later, the door came apart as if someone on the outside pulled it outward. Before we realized it, Baldreek jumped out of the transport, ran, and yelled back at us to follow him.

He stopped briefly and threw small smoke bombs on the ground before grabbing our hands and running again. A thick smoke ignited, spreading and making it hard for all to see clearly. Even though my body quivered from a chilliness that I didn't have an explanation for, I proceeded to run with Baldreek because of his strong grip. I detested him for pulling us back into the distress of chasings after we'd lived tranquilly for four days, almost forgetting what we were going through.

The amount of smoke that clouded us as we ran was impressive, considering how much remained for a long distance after being ignited from small balls. We stopped when Shadia screamed, falling to the ground.

"I'll carry you!" Baldreek said. She protested, but it seemed like he didn't pay much attention to her response because he lifted her anyway. He asked me to hold on to his arm so we wouldn't lose each other. I didn't know how long we ran, but when we finally ended up in another vehicle, I was completely out of breath.

The transport started moving as Baldreek said, "We're running out of time! It's clear that they have new technologies to track outlaws. If anything happens to me, you have to head to the fifth cave north from the waterfall, in the direction that we're moving. My group and I are trying our best to help you escape. In that cave, you'll find what will help you do so. In case of any emergency, head back to the shelter and press the survival button, temporarily giving in to your kidnappers. My group and I will find a way to get you and help you escape."

"Escape where?" I cautiously asked. If he was speaking the truth, did that mean that his activist comrades possessed governmental technologies that were advanced enough to help us travel through space?

"We have supporters in intricate and sensitive places, and they will return you to Earth no matter the price. Not just you... There are hundreds of Earthlings undergoing similar testing."

"I still don't get what the point of the experiments is if the religious faction publicly says they don't intend to return to Earth!" I said.

"The public reason for the tests is to select superior humans who carry the best genetic qualities. Those qualities don't become clear unless you put humans under an immense environmental pressure—not just by using DNA that was studied in some lab."

Baldreek also added that even though that was the public reason, there was some secret chatter going on about a deal between the religious government and the opposing government that offered both options: whoever wanted to travel to Earth would have that opportunity, and whoever decided to stay on Editia would benefit from the best male mating samples—to impregnate females from their planet—to bring forth a healthy, genetically-improved generation, or at least a genetic treatment.

My head spun with details, but Shadia and I continued to ask questions. He answered them while explaining his plans along the way. Suddenly there were a number of uninterrupted explosions outside the vehicle and then the sound of a loud buzzing, after which our ride became dark. Another explosion blew the door of the transport away, and before we could jump from it, about five harpoons were shot our way. All of them penetrated Baldreek's body, making him wince in pain, then he lay completely still.

14

Zahra sighed in boredom as she got up from her desk to walk around in her exam room. Her legs were stiff from sitting all day. She held the remote control for the examination table and kept raising and lowering the bed, reclining the back and making it upright again to pass the time. For the third day in a row, not one patient had knocked on her clinic's door. Her assistant's reasoning was that during this particular month, the number of patients was usually lower than the rest of the months, but it was an unconvincing excuse. Her patients were rare either way.

Zahra lived in a society that still disapproved the idea of a female surgeon. When she worked at her university's hospital, some people, especially men, expressed their concern at the idea of letting a loved one undergo surgery performed by a female doctor. Many times a person solicited a male doctor to do the surgery instead of her, and that person would display astonishment mixed with displeasure when they found out that she was the supervisor of that male doctor—she was the one who taught him how to hold a scalpel. That was a common incident in the hospital's university. As for her private clinic, it was even rarer for people to take a chance and undergo a surgery she'd perform, especially since she specialized in neurosurgery.

Her assistant knocked on the door and informed her there was someone who wanted to meet her regarding a hospitalized patient. She allowed a dark, slim young man with a crooked nose to enter and he sat on the chair in front of her. He began to talk awkwardly.

"I have a relative who suffers from severe burns. He's between life and death, and he needs your help."

Zahra raised her eyebrows in surprise. "What does my specialty have to do with burns?"

The man sipped some water and said, "I don't get it either, but it's the patient's wish. He mentioned that he knew someone called Dr. Zahra who specializes in relieving pain through injecting the nerves, and that it was the only way to help him."

She was happy to learn that! Somewhere a patient specifically requested her by name to benefit from her method of treating pain. Not many people knew she had mastered that technique except a small number of fellow doctors.

The man added, "You helped a friend of this person who used to have cancer. Your method soothed his pains and helped him live his last days in peace. This patient is called Omar Awadallah, who's hospitalized in Al-salam Specialized Hospital in the critical burns department."

Before getting up, he asked about her fees. "The secretary outside will inform you of those details.

But first, let his doctor give me a call." The man thanked her and left.

Minutes later, she received a phone call from Sameh, Omar's doctor. He explained the case to her and added, "I was surprised when my patient told me about you; I always thought that relieving pain this way is an anesthesiologist's specialty, not a neurosurgeon's."

"It was the thesis for my PhD. I mastered it and became known in my university for that specific method of relieving pain," she said.

That PhD topic was initially forced on her by her supervisor, who didn't want to give her an intricate field—like the surgery of brain tumors—to write about. Similar to the rest of her professors, he thought that her training in neurosurgery was a big mistake, so he tried to limit her by restricting her interest to other specialties under the umbrella of "widening her perspective of neurosurgical concentrations." But she mastered the art of relieving pain to the extent that her anesthesiologist colleagues sometimes asked for her opinion with their more challenging cases. But that still didn't stop her from practicing surgeries on spinal columns and brains, especially ones caused by accidents.

At the scheduled appointment, Zahra immediately felt that Omar looked somewhat familiar to her, like an actor or celebrity, or one of her colleagues, even. She asked if they'd met before.

"We met when you were treating my friend, and I talked to you back then."

Sameh brought her everything she needed while she unpacked the medication she would inject the nerves with. She informed Omar that he was lucky that his back was fine, because it would allow her to apply anesthesia to the sensory nerves for his stomach and thighs. It was going to be trickier to perform the procedure for his arms because his neck was all burned.

He thanked her for her efforts and asked about the duration of the injections.

"The session will be no longer than thirty minutes."

"You misunderstood me. I mean, how long will the injection effects stay?"

"Around three months."

He thought about it for a while, then said, "Great, let's do it!" But he sounded like he was hiding something.

***

Zahra began to inject the nerves that connected to his lower right limb. She gave him a small shot, which made him groan, but she assured him that he was not going to feel any more pain and patted his back with her gloved hand. The gesture made him feel an unusual tranquility. Something moved underneath his skin, then a heavy, liquid rush flowed from the end of the syringe. Suddenly, the pain from his burns completely disappeared from his right leg, and the ease extended to his thigh.

After Zahra made sure it worked on him successfully, she moved to inject his lower left limb as well. However, he asked her to give him some time to rest.

Sameh frowned and attempted to rush him, but Zahra said, "You can leave if you want. I'll stay with Mr. Omar until he calms down, then we can proceed."

So Sameh left them while Zahra sat on the chair next to Omar, who was being helped by the nurse to turn and rest on his back.

Omar thanked her for coming, expressing his astonishment at how the pain in his right side had completely vanished, flattering and complimenting her skills. She seemed to feel shy and humbly thanked him, saying she hoped he got well soon.

"I know I only have a limited amount of time here, but all I wanted was to see you before I die," he said. She looked perplexed, so he altered his words. "I meant so that you could make my pain stop."

She asked for the reason behind his burns.

"It's a long story. I'm actually writing it down as a book so it will be known after I die."

She adjusted herself on the shabby chair, then asked him for the reason he spoke of death so uncaringly, and why he had given up hope altogether.

"I brought in a well-known doctor for consultation and he told me that this is most likely going to end in my passing. It's only a matter of time, so I don't want to take too long overthinking it. Death will come sooner or later.

"I think of life as a rented house: Its owner leases it to you for a specific amount of time, then kicks you out. You should be fine with getting kicked out, especially if you surpassed the contract duration. It's a disgusting house with many problems—its walls are cracked, the plumbing is faulty, the power frequently goes out, and the neighbors are hostile and throw their garbage at your house from time to time."

She smiled at his analogy, so he proceeded. "Then there are the streets! Crammed, crowded, noisy, full of fights and car exhaust." She laughed with him. "The owner of the house let me live there for almost forty years and didn't make me leave. It was only after a beautiful jasmine tree started growing outside of the house, giving me a sense of a real home; that the owner said I could merely remain until the end of the month because I'd overstayed my welcome."

Curious, she asked, "What do you do, Omar?"

"I'm plumber with a degree in history, and I'm an obscure novelist!"

"Are you joking?"

"No, I swear I am speaking the truth. I do have a furnished apartment, and I would love to settle down if you know someone looking for a husband."

She laughed. "Are you always that funny, or is it perhaps the kind of gallows humor caused by depression?"

She summoned the nurse to prepare him so she could proceed with what she'd started, but he asked her to call it a day.

"We have to carry on!" she insisted. "I won't be available to come all this distance again soon."

"I will get my relative to pay for two more visits in advance."

"It's not about the money," she said. "The usual routine is to inject everything all at once."

She eventually gave in to his persistence and agreed to visit him in two days to carry on, under the condition that he would let her finish the following time. He thanked her genuinely and reached out his bandaged hand to say goodbye. She briefly hesitated, then accepted so she wouldn't hurt his feelings or make him think she was repulsed by his wounded hand. They shook hands, and to her surprise, she felt his warm fingertips pressing gently on her wrist. She didn't attempt to explain his behavior. He was a patient with a critical, severe case of burns, and he could only be trying to express his gratitude.

Before she left, he asked her to open the drawer of the nightstand next to his bed. When she asked for the reason, he pleadingly asked her again to do it.

"What do you want from the drawer?" she asked.

"Take this red flash drive," he said. "It contains what I've written so far in my novel about the reasons behind my injuries. I hope you can read it soon."

"I'm not used to digital reading."

"Then I'll print it out and give you a copy the day after tomorrow."

"No need. I'll read it from the memory stick as soon as I find the time."

He thanked her again in a quavering voice. His eyes shone with tears as he told her that she could never imagine the kind of help she gave him.

15

It was the first time I witnessed someone dying, and it was at that same moment that I realized Baldreek was not fooling us. It wasn't a part of the game. For me, the idea of death was represented by the image of a person on their deathbed, their lips smiling and eyes half-closed. You already knew that they had passed away, and it was your chance to take one last look at them.

When my dad died, I was studying in college. He was taking his usual nap, but Mom went into his room to wake him up and he didn't respond. My mom passed away in the intensive care unit after a brain stroke. She remained in the hospital for a week before they eventually called me at dawn from the hospital and informed me of her death. They also told me I was required to make arrangements for her corpse, and requested me to pay the rest of the hospital bill.

When Baldreek's body became still, I automatically assumed he'd died, but when Shadia checked, she claimed that he wasn't dead. She opened his bag, removed a syringe that looked like the one he used earlier, and injected him with it. That was smart and courageous of her; perhaps that behavior was ignited by her belief that we were safe and that our kidnappers wouldn't sacrifice our lives.

The man took a deep breath, then bit his thick lips in pain. Only then did I regain my confidence. I tried to take one of the harpoons out of Baldreek's thigh, but he shrieked, so I stopped.

"Leave me and quickly run to the cave I told you about. There you'll find people who will take you off the island. Remember that if anything goes wrong, press the survival button and head to the shelter. Remain there until you are taken by those who will set you free."

Shadia held his hand and said that we weren't going to leave him, but Baldreek told her to stop arguing about it.

"No!" she said. "Just let us know how we can help."

"I agree—we're not going to leave you here to die," I said.

The man smiled, but suddenly his breathing became rapid and heavy. He began drooling and his eyes rolled backward.

Shadia opened his bag and asked him, in between aggressively shaking him to keep him awake, "Which injection should I use? The first one didn't help!"

Baldreek replied with overlapping sounds that didn't make any sense. She got out a second syringe and plunged it into his shoulder. He didn't move for the first couple of seconds, then his breathing became rapid, but sounded shallow. It didn't seem the air was reaching his lungs.

The man died in front of us and I cried my eyes out. I leaned my back onto the remains of the vehicle and covered my face in my hands. As for Shadia, she closed Baldreek's eyes, then furiously hit the vehicle's base, yelling words that didn't make sense. As soon as she calmed down, she put her hand on my shoulder and patted it, and when I didn't react, she firmly grabbed my arm and pulled my hands away from my face. "Now is not the time, Omar—we have to leave. Pull yourself together and let's go!"

Our roles were reversed that time. She regained her self-control and I had collapsed. She was thinking on her feet and I was uncertain. In several previous situations, she was more opinionated and her suggestions were more precise than mine. She possessed the skill to analyze the situation, while I became anxious and clung to the first decision that crossed my mind. That was typical of me, as I often hesitated and lost track of my direction under pressure. That time specifically she made me feel like a lost child...that she was coaxing me out of hiding and taking me back to the playground.

I gazed at her and at her warm face, then pulled my arm away from her hand. For some reason I didn't know at the time, I kissed her forehead. I thanked her and got up. Her face was taut from my action, so I immediately apologized, but she didn't respond. She stepped away from the vehicle's remains and I followed. We rapidly walked in the direction of the mountain, with trees to our right and the river to our left.

Shadia suddenly stopped. She stared at me silently for a few moments and opened her mouth to say something, then pursed her lips. Without speaking, she turned her back on me and continued rushing ahead.

Our steps became faster as we approached the mountain. I was wondering what was going on in her head. My kiss didn't mean anything—it was just an expression of my gratitude toward her presence, or... Maybe it expressed some bottled-up feelings. I didn't really know, but I knew for a fact that no other woman was able handle me that way during my fragile moments. Actually, I had never allowed myself to express private or fragile moments in front of a woman before, not a girlfriend or a wife. I never thought that a woman deserved to see me cry.

Perhaps the only reason I allowed myself to cry in front of her was that we were alone in a world with no real human beings, struggling to remain safe yet being crushed in an absurd game controlled by a bunch of people who treated us like livestock. Or should I say that they were *merely selecting the more superior lines for mating...* If the dead man whose corpse we left rotting in the forest spoke the truth.

I asked her what she intended to do and why she retreated. She didn't reply and walked even faster.

"I'm sorry about the kiss! I will never do that again," I said.

"Please stop talking until we know what we're going to do. Then we'll have plenty of time to talk."

She was right. Our sole means of survival could diminish if we were late. Our rescuers could be attacked by those sensors, or they could have a pack of wolves or a flood or something of the sort sent to them.

We arrived at the waterfall. We began to walk north, counting the cave openings we saw. We counted two, but the third was a source of disagreement. It looked like only a small gap in the mountain, but I insisted it was the third entrance and that we only had to pass one more, then enter the following one. Shadia insisted that this small one shouldn't be counted at all. We passed by the following cave. Then we saw, right next to it, another cave that was much larger than all its precedents. I immediately knew that was the intended one.

Shadia didn't argue and we entered together. I walked in front of her and she slowly roamed around, exploring the walls. Abruptly she stopped moving and signaled me to do the same.

She pointed to a thin part in the wall that looked like it could be a possible place for a door that they controlled. Perhaps our captors would close it after we entered, like they did before. I froze in place, not knowing what the next step was. She suggested we explore the next cave, but I refused to leave before knowing if there was anyone waiting at the other end of this cave or not. I told her to wait for me outside, as I decided to walk until I reached the end of the cave and return quickly. She tried to object, but I didn't give her the chance and marched away quickly.

The cave grew narrower the deeper I went. When I started to feel that the distance might be much longer than what I surmised, I stopped for a moment to think. *If they want to help us escape, they would have picked a wider cave, and they probably own tools to help them know all about the existing caves, like those doors and the traps.* I decided to go back and began to run toward the entrance.

I sprinted faster when I heard Shadia's screams—especially when there were also animal noises I couldn't identify. The racket was mixed with Shadia's screaming. I reached the entrance to find her with her back turned against the cave's wall while two animals fought in front of her. They resembled smaller versions of leopards but battled each other viciously, barely paying any attention to us. I took her hand to lead her out of there, but she whispered to me not to move so they wouldn't shift their attention to us.

"They are too busy. They didn't even notice your screaming," I whispered back.

So we left the cave…only to find a whole family of bystander predators watching the fight and not paying any attention us.

It was only natural to return to the cave. As soon as the battle ended, we were going to become their feast. As one of the leopards showed more superiority in his combat skills, I grabbed Shadia by the hand and ran deeper into the cave. She followed me, protesting.

"Dying at the hands of those predators is inevitable, but getting doors closed on us is worse," I said.

"Those beasts could be trained—they could be part of the game! For example, we didn't see any wolves after that first pack. They seem to have disappeared from the whole island!"

Her words would have made more sense if I hadn't seen blood dripping from the defeated animal. No creature sacrificed its life in obedience to a trainer. The survival instinct is stronger than anything else for all beings, except for humans. Stupidity sometimes came first.

The beasts' sounds became clearer inside the tunnel. Evidently the battle was over and it was time to celebrate by devouring a human feast. The tunnel still extended as we ran until we reached the end, and the sea appeared through an opening. I looked through and noticed that the ledge was narrower than the one on the other side of the waterfall, and this opening was higher.

The savage noises became louder and got closer. I knew Shadia normally lost her composure with animals, starting from rats all the way to leopards, and she would lose her strong, decision-making personality.

I told her to squirm through the hole, and then I would hold her arm until she came close to the ledge so she could land safely on it. She hesitated at first. Then the sounds got even louder and more frequent, so she obeyed. I held on to her suspended body as firmly and dangled her down as far as I could, but her feet were still almost one meter away from the ledge. She was afraid to fall, lose her balance, and end up in the water. My arm was almost breaking from holding on to her. The animals became quiet and I only heard their pads on the floor, and I knew that they were very close. I begged her to let go so I could jump after her.

She screamed frantically and closed her eyes while letting go of my hand. At that exact same moment, something bit my leg. Without thinking, I leaped away from the excruciating pain and a large cat jumped with me, still with his jaw latched onto my leg.

The three of us ended up in the deep water with the waves pulling us in while Shadia and the cat struggled not to drown. I grasped her with determination and fought the waves, which were fortunately not that strong. I reached the ledge, held on to it and helped her climb up, then followed her.

The struggling animal trying not to drown also wanted to reach the ledge. I considered helping it, as it seemed like a poor, helpless, newborn cat amid an overwhelming tide, but I took one look at the blood on my leg and backed off. I looked at Shadia and she evidently felt pity for it as well. I thought about helping it again, but then I heard a loud uproar, similar to a sports car motor.

Above the water, a ship that looked like a spaceship in science fiction movies appeared. It was the size of a four-wheel-drive car, but it was pointy in the front and slightly crooked on the sides, with a slight curve. The door opened and a man stood there, looking similar to Baldreek, who died a while earlier. He held the helm between his hands and signaled for us to wait. Then he moved the ship, trying to get lower and dropping close to the ledge, but it seemed somewhat complicated.

He made the ship rise, then got close to the mountain and began to descend right above us. His maneuvering apparently triggered some sort of sensor because a missile shot toward the vehicle from somewhere in the mountain and struck the front.

16

Flying shrapnel was dispersed from the front of the ship, and one piece even flew right by me. I expected the ship to spin in circles and swirl for some time, then fall down, burning us along with it and providing freedom from our agony once and for all. However, none of that happened. Unexpectedly, a number of luminous balls were released from the sides of the ship, swirling in random directions. The captain of the ship then attempted to come back once again.

A missile was fired, but one of the luminous balls caught it, absorbed it, and flew far away with it. A second, then third missile was fired and the same thing happened. At that point, Shadia and I realized that our defenders were proficient and that we were finally about to escape. I held her hand and helped her climb the small ladder that descended from the ship. The rate of fired missiles increased as Shadia climbed inside and I began to scramble up the ladder.

Another group of missiles were shot at once, one of which succeeded in missing the balls and hitting the side close to the ladder. The vehicle lost its balance and I fell back on the ledge, feeling dizzy, as if part of my head were being torn apart. The ship took off rapidly, carrying Shadia and avoiding the rest of the missiles.

For a moment, different thoughts in my head conflicted with one another. Shadia was going to escape. If they managed to save me as well, great. If they didn't, I would have to complete my time, undergo some experiments, give them what they wanted, and then return. Was I truly going to stay in that place for three whole years to write down my diaries, or would they cut my time short, drag me to the lab, run their experiments on me—perhaps collect my sperm to fertilize their women with it—and then let me go?

What if they were planning to keep me there with them? Was I going to abandon my home and the people whom I knew all my life and live with new traditions, beliefs, and strangers who didn't even follow my religion? But really, why would that be a problem? I could potentially discover that people there were more decent, more sophisticated, or less likely to deceive or exploit others. The laws could be more humane and traditions more plausible. In addition, my identity would be entirely different from the one I bore on Earth. On Editia, I was not going to be just another ordinary person—I was going to be an Earthling.

If they decided to keep me there, I would be privileged and receive special treatment. They would find me one of their women to marry so they could acquire a new breed. Perhaps it wouldn't be too enjoyable if the women had unpleasant features, but I would get used to it. With time, maybe I could find beauty in their features that I didn't notice at first.

I would bring tens of newborns to life, maybe hundreds, and I wouldn't be responsible for their care. If any of them contacted a disease, I wouldn't carry the responsibility of raising them or paying for their school tuitions or handling their failures in life. I wouldn't have to save money to marry my daughters or spend money on my unemployed sons. My offspring would be of an elite class: they were going to be treated in a special manner, not to mention I was going to save planet Earth from being partially occupied by prehistoric Neanderthals.

All those thoughts buzzed in my head as I lay on the rocks with my eyes closed—an injured leg, a bruised head, and a half-conscious brain. Many thoughts intermingled with one another, then I had to confront the main idea I was trying to avoid: I was going to live in that place without Shadia. Despite her personality and attitude, Shadia was a basic anchor for me to survive in that exile. My heart sank when I thought about her leaving, but I tried to push that feeling away and replace it with plans for a new life on that planet.

I heard the same loud sound again—the one produced by that flying ship, a sports car engine. I opened my eyes and saw it approaching me once more, with its door open and Shadia waving at me, yelling my name so loudly that it overcame the sound of the ship. The luminous balls protecting the ship were fired anew and the captain flew as close to me as he possibly could. I was barely able to pull myself together, but I grabbed the ladder, which was loose now, and began to climb. Shadia reached out her hand and helped me get in at the same moment that tens of harpoons were released toward the ship. They missed us, but struck the captain's head and neck as if they were being moved by a PlayStation controller.

The man was killed with his hand still fixed on the ship's helm, which made it sharply tilt and fall in the water. I expected we would drown as it created a whirlpool to drag us toward the bottom, but luckily, it floated. I didn't waste any time in thinking: I jumped in the water as Shadia clung to me and we swam to the ledge. It was a small distance, barely five meters. She held on to my back as I swam in the warm water, which was only very slightly salty, but bitter. It tasted like diluted lemon juice added to a spoon of salt.

I felt a strange sense of warmth on my back where she held me. The warmth vanished for a few seconds, than rapidly returned. I asked her if she wanted to come back to the island with me, or was she truly relieved to leave that prison? She said sharply, "Now is not the time!"

I laughed and said, "I was going to miss that sharp tongue."

We rested on the ledge. I was overcome with exhaustion, so I asked if we could catch our breath for some time before thinking about our next step. Two individuals died trying to save us, which made me wonder if they would send others who were willing to sacrifice their lives.

"They won't try again," said Shadia. "At the end of the day, we're nothing but a cause to them. I don't think defending that cause is worth dying for."

"Numerous people give up their lives to save victims they don't personally know," I said. "Foreign activists in occupied Palestine do it regularly. Rachel Corrie[12] got killed defending a Palestinian house without being aware of its owners' tendencies."

"I'm not interested in politics. Especially not in the Palestinian problem."

I didn't argue with her—it wasn't worth the time. It was vital to think of ourselves.

Shadia added, "I feel guilty about the ship's captain. I insisted we go back and get you. I couldn't move forward without you."

I smiled, but my expression soon faded when she said that Baldreek didn't deserve to die for my sake, and that nothing was going to happen if she'd left me here. She thought I was a cat, with nine lives.

I always behaved that way with the opposite sex as well. I killed any emotional moment and destroyed any romantic feeling before it could develop. I did it because of my fear of the opposite sex, the fear of getting truly attached to a woman, then becoming exposed to pain because of my love. I didn't, however, think that way when it came to Shadia. She wasn't as much of a "woman" as a companion who happened to be a woman. She was hot-tempered yet soft and sympathetic, intelligent yet shallow, and a decision-maker yet all over the place. She didn't speak much about herself, except for that one time

---

[12] Rachel Aliene Corrie: An American peace activist who was killed while trying to stop an Israeli army bulldozer from demolishing a Palestinian home in the Gaza Strip (1979–2003).

when she opened up about a failed love story. I had closed the door on her then, so she didn't continue.

"You take the lead," I told her. She shrugged in confusion, not knowing what to do. There were only two days left in the grace period. I wondered what they intended to do with us after this all came to an end.

Will they leave us here to rot or subject us to more tests? And how long will we stay alive before they decide that the experiment has officially come to an end and they must eliminate the Earthlings?

Shadia said, "Maybe our way out of here is a flying ship, like the one we were just in, not a regular one. It could be hidden somewhere in the forest, not necessarily on the beach. Assuming the location means we could look for it for an entire year and find nothing. It might even be camouflaged or hidden in a way that makes it extremely hard to find!" Then she said jokingly, "If I knew for a fact that the shelter contained clean clothes, I would head there right away!" She touched her clothes—still not clean despite all the times we got wet.

I suggested we go back to the tunnel, enter the shelter, and wait like Baldreek told us to. She said, "We have to get moving anyway. We can't stay here on the rocks! But how are we going to cross the river where we left our tents and the bags?"

She got up and asked me to keep shuffling along the ledge to the part opposite to the falls, then carry on until we found a cave that led back to the forest. I listened, rose, and speedily yet cautiously walked ahead. We reached the part that stuck out of the mountain, which met the waterfall on the inside.

The ledge was too thin there; it was difficult just to stand on. I told her we would have to swim past that section in the water, but she stood in her place, refusing to move.

She leaned her back against the wall and sat down in defeat, gazing at the sky and the sun that was about to set. I entreated her to carry on, but she began to mumble, "I'm sick of this game. How long is this going to carry on?"

As she pleadingly asked God for help, I sat next to her and patted her shoulder. "God won't let us down."

"Do you pray, Omar?"

I was taken aback. We were going through so much, it didn't even occur to me to pray on that different planet.

I remembered studying fiqh[13] during my Islamic high school years, and how the professors created the most unlikely scenarios and presented their interpretations. My colleagues and I used to make fun of the abundance of improbable scenarios, but our professors said that the whole field of fiqh is built on assumption.

Well, then... Did any of the fiqh scholars or their students ever envision a scenario like the one we were in at the moment? I brushed it off, telling Shadia that we were forgiven from not praying. First

---

[13] Fiqh (in Arabic فقه): The study of Islamic jurisprudence. It is the human understanding of Islamic law as revealed in the Quran and the Sunnah.

of all, there was no qibla[14] in that place, and if the place didn't exist, the result consequently vanished as well. She didn't understand what I said and asked me to further explain it, but I asked her not to bother me. She couldn't understand my religious ideologies...and I didn't understand what I was saying either.

"To make a long story short, I am the professional mufti[15] on this planet, and I'm telling you we don't have to pray here. But we will compensate for the missing prayers when we return to Earth." I spoke in a serious voice, resembling those sheikhs who spoke on the radio.

She laughed sarcastically. "You're the last person to be a sheikh or give rulings on religious matters, even though your beard has lately grown very long. It makes you look like one!"

Our foolery somewhat improved her mood, and she eventually listened and agreed to get in the water. I entered the water first. She held on to the ledge with her left hand and wrapped her right arm around my chest, apparently intending to hug me. I swam slowly until we moved past the tricky area with no ledge, then I continued swimming—instead of scaling up to the ledge—until we reached the bottom of the cave that we were captured in before.

---

[14] Qibla (in Arabic قبلة): The direction in toward the Kaaba, a Sacred Mosque in Mecca, used to determine the direction of prayer by Muslims in various religious contexts.

[15] Mufti (in Arabic مفتي): An Islamic legal authority who gives a legal opinion on a point of Islamic law.

We both climbed and I supported her until she reached the opening, then she reached out her hand to help me scramble up. We settled in the cave, and she suggested that we rest for a while. I disagreed and asked her to quickly cross to the other side so they wouldn't close the door on us.

"That round of the game is over. They won't close it again," she said. After thinking about it, though, she decided I had a point. We could drink some water and eat fruit there, for we were both starved and dehydrated.

17

The corridor that connected the burn unit to the hospital's main gate was quite long, or so Zahra thought as she walked along quickly after refusing Sameh's offer to accompany her. She almost bumped into two strangers accidentally on her way to the exit, where she finally arrived at the large reception area that contained the hospital's entrance.

She felt a strange and unexplainable sense of bliss. She naturally resisted it with an instinctual fear at first, then she was overwhelmed with skepticism and contemplated the reason behind her feeling. She eventually gave in. It was the kind of pleasant feeling that followed a heartwarming experience, like after her graduation ceremony, or after the first surgery she performed by herself, or after the first kiss her first fiancé gave her on the cheek. (Even though things between them later went downhill, that moment never lost its glory.)

She arrived at the spot where she parked her car, but it wasn't there. She looked to her left and right to no avail. She asked the security man staffing that parking area. He asked if she possibly left the car in a different spot. Then she remembered that she indeed parked it on the other side, so she thanked him and returned, eventually finding her car in a different parking place.

The drive between the hospital in Al Salam City to her house in Nasr City took almost an hour, at least half of which was spent in traffic jams. She sprayed some air freshener, started the car, and the voice of Abdelghani El Sayed[16] sang "Al Helwa W Al Mora." It was the first song in a playlist she'd put together that did not appeal to anyone but her. She adored a certain type of singers that weren't loved except by people who had an acquired taste, like Karem Mohamed, Moharam Fouad, Souad Mohamed, and Fayed Mohamed Fayed.[17]

She never genuinely enjoyed nineties music, even though she listened to it during her teenage years. She didn't, however, fall in love with Kazem Al Saher[18] and Amr Diab's[19] voices, and she never understood musical trends that began on Facebook either—like underground bands, for instance. Her love for neglected artists was equal to her appreciation of anything abandoned, or anyone that people gave less than their true value. When she was still a student, she was a clever, popular, and outstanding girl, loved by everyone. Even then, she appreciated anything on the sidelines, especially when it came to music.

When she started her neurosurgeon residency, however, everyone turned against her and tried to

---

[16] Abdelghani El Sayed (in Arabic السيد عبد الغنى): An Egyptian singer (1908–1962).

[17] Prominent Egyptian singers who rose to fame in the 1950s.

[18] Kazem Al Saher (in Arabic كاظم الساهر): An Iraqi singer and songwriter known for his romantic ballads.

[19] Amr Diab (in Arabic عمرو دياب): An Egyptian popstar; singer, composer, and actor.

bring her down just for being a female—as if women didn't fit that specialty. If she misjudged something, people made mountains out of molehills; if she achieved success, no one mentioned it. She began to feel sidelined herself and grew even softer toward underdogs, since she became one.

He's a strange man. He knows his time is coming, yet he insists on writing a novel for other people to read. Why isn't he thinking about anything else? she wondered as she recalled the sound of Omar's voice, struggling to speak, begging her to read what he wrote. She was considering it, even though she didn't enjoy reading anything since her PhD exams. A sense of familiarity toward him existed that she didn't understand. It seemed as though their conversations took her back to forgotten better days.

It occurred to her that he only refused to continue his treatment the first time so she would go and visit him again, but that was a strange thought that made no sense. No one who felt that kind of physical pain would refuse to be fully treated just to meet some woman, no matter who she was. She briefly smiled as the thought appealed to her femininity, but she soon pushed it away, saying out loud, "What is this nonsense?!" right before slamming on the brakes to avoid crashing into a young man who drove his car past hers to switch to the left lane. She cursed both him and traffic laws before she carried on. She couldn't curse anyone before she started to work as a surgeon: only after did she gain that "beneficial" skill.

While waiting in a long traffic-light line, she caught her own face in the front mirror and put some of the loose hair strands back underneath her headscarf. For the first time, she noticed the fine lines around her eyes and between her eyebrows. She anxiously bit her lips. She turned thirty-six few days before, and rejected a potential suitor who was introduced to her by her professor's wife. The woman was mad that Zahra refused him and made an unnecessary comment about how a woman her age should not be rejecting men. She needed to keep in mind her diminishing ability to bear children.

Omar popped in her head again and she remembered how he looked her. Men look at people differently, and any woman can tell which is which. It wasn't suggestive, flirty, or tacky, but more of a genuine look. The kind of look that started in the heart and then settled behind his eyes just to look at her. She had never seen a look similar to that one. It was capable of drawing a smile from her soul and throwing a pebble in her dry pond of feelings, which shook its composed surface.

A while back, she was driving on an empty, dark back road—one that she was used to taking to avoid traffic—and she got in a car accident. A long time passed before she was found and taken to a hospital, unconscious. She woke up in the MRI machine, dressed in hospital clothes, not knowing when or how they were put on her. She felt like a maniac for an entire day, as she couldn't talk or think normally. It was the first time for her to experience a concussion, which she was used to diagnosing her patients with on an almost weekly basis. She was the one experiencing it that time, and it made her perceive it differently.

After the accident, she began to feel like she was missing something in her life...some sort of gap within her. With every passing day, she felt like there was something she was compelled to do, but she didn't know what. That feeling especially intensified at nighttime, before she went to bed. She would get up many times and fiddle with something random: scroll through her phone after having turned it off, go into her kitchen to make sure the fridge still worked, call a friend on the phone to ask for a favor, and so on.

Her peers at work explained they were post-concussion symptoms and that they would go away on their own with the passing of time. Her thoughts, however, never went away—except during those short minutes spent with her strange patient. The one who admired her for no good reason and decided to endure additional pain just to see her again, even though he had little time left in this world.

**

At that moment, Omar was in the wound dressing room. Sameh was cleaning the wounds in his usual aggressive manner, but Omar didn't feel any kind of pain on the side that Zahra sedated. Sameh was working with unusual ease before he began cleaning the other side. Omar immediately went back to shrieking in pain. Sameh scolded him and said he was solely responsible for enduring the pain since he refused to have Dr. Zahra finish both sides.

Nothing can distract a person from the pain of getting a burn wound cleaned, no matter how distracted or elated you feel.

Omar realized that fact the moment Sameh began to clean the wounds on his arms. Despite that, his pain lessened somewhat, or rather, the emotional torment that accompanied the physical one. Contrary to what many people think, emotional distress does not cause physical pain as much as the other way around, especially from a frequent source. Every day, the physical agony during wound dressing ate at a part of his soul. Before it could heal, the suffering returned the following day and made the damage deeper and more severe. Only on that day, the relief from the earlier visit was sufficient to fill the gap in his soul and protect it from aftermath of pain. All he felt was the physical torment.

After Sameh finished Omar's dressing, he allowed him to sit in a chair for some time outside the intensive care unit. Omar noticed the same two boys playing in the corridor. He called out for them, so they ran to him, racing each other as fast as they could. He laughed at their behavior, reminding himself that burns, war, or anything in the world wasn't able to assassinate the innocence of childhood.

"I'm going to ask you both a question, and whoever gets it right gets a present from me," he said.

"I'm sure it's candy, as usual!" said the smaller kid. Omar laughed and told them that it was going to be different that time.

"I will tell you a story, then quiz you on the events."

"Ask away, Mr. Omar," said the older kid.

Omar laughed again, but insisted that they must bring chairs and listen carefully. Then he began to tell them one of the stories that his grandfather used to tell him: a beautiful young girl named Aaishaa who was oppressed by her stepmother. The older woman stole Aaishaa's lover to marry him to her own daughter, and resorted to using an evil ogress to help her.

The smaller boy said he'd heard a similar story on a kids TV channel. "But the little girl was called Cinderella."

"No! My story is purely Egyptian," Omar said. "No one calls an ogress Omena Al Ghola[20] except in Egyptian stories. The similarity between the two stories stems from the image of the evil stepmother, which is common in all cultures."

The kids didn't understand a word, but he carried on with his stories. He asked them questions and they answered, so Omar told one of the janitors to bring him a bag that was next to his bed.

He removed two toys and gave one to each of them. It was a device similar to a tablet, with a strong, protective cover. The kids walked away with their presents happily after being asked to pray for their Uncle Omar. Sameh, who was standing there and witnessed the event, asked him for the price of those devices, and was astonished to hear it.

"When I asked Dr. Hend about the best way to decrease those kids' physical pain, she told me that

---

[20] Omena Al Ghola (in Arabic أمنا الغولة): A famous Egyptian mythical character known for scaring and kidnapping children.

in some Western countries, they bring tablet-like devices to the kids to distract them during wound dressings. I asked her to look for a way to buy those devices, and she did."

"So, I take it that plumbing pays well!" Sameh said, being facetious. Omar nodded.

"I have an okay amount of money in my bank account. But my days are limited, and soon I won't possess anything except for a heartfelt prayer from those kids."

Sameh told him to get back to bed and asked him to fight his despair. "Some foreign expert is attending a conference here in Cairo. He might respond to the medical director's invitation and come visit the hospital to check on some cases, including yours. Until then, don't lose hope."

18

I ate half the fruit in one bite after I realized its sweet flavor was similar to pears. At that moment, the taste reminded me of the food served during funeral ceremonies in our village, where you'd devour your food because you'd been exhausted and starving all day long. Your taste buds would savor its deliciousness, but you still felt guilty because someone just died and you should be mourning his death instead of enjoying your food. Sometimes I let go of my guilt and gave in to enjoying the food because I was certain that some women in my village flourished in preparing specific funeral foods.

In contrast, Shadia barely finished one piece of fruit. Her eyes welled up with tears as she dropped what remained and muttered words I didn't understand. It was already nighttime, but one of the moons had vanished. We couldn't walk in any direction after our long day, so we rested on the grass near the riverbank. Two men had lost their lives to set us free. If we'd been kidnapped on Earth, no one would do that.

"We're going to get through this! Those men died for a noble cause that they both believed in. None of this is our fault. We didn't choose to be kidnapped, and we didn't choose to be saved either," I told Shadia.

She laid down on her back on the grass. "How do you know I feel guilty?"

"Because I feel the same way!" I was trying to console myself as much as I was trying to console her by saying those words.

She wanted me to change the subject. "Imagine that we are two strangers who randomly met on a tourist island. What would you talk to me about?"

I laughed. "I'm the last man on Earth who can initiate a conversation with a woman. I only tried a couple of times back in my day, and failed miserably. So how about you tell me more about yourself instead?" I laid on the grass on my back next to her.

She thought about it for a few seconds, then said, "Nothing in my life is worth mentioning."

I couldn't help but feel frustrated. After all we had been through, she still treated me like a stranger. I knew that ten, or even twenty, days weren't sufficient to make us the closest of friends, but we were alone in a strange world, and it was possible that we could stay that way forever. So how long were we going to remain strangers?

I fought those thoughts, went back to my regular state of mind, and simply reminded myself that my luck with women was never successful. I told myself that if we were meant to survive and leave, I would probably never see her face again.

She didn't speak for a while, so I assumed she went to sleep and I attempted to do the same. Then I heard her sigh. I was about to ask her what was keeping her awake, but the question sounded dumb in my head, so I prevented myself from asking so she wouldn't respond cynically. She was lying almost three meters away from me. She turned left and right a couple of times, then got up and walked in the direction of the trees.

"Where to?" I asked.

"After ten days together in the open space and you're still asking that question?" she said sarcastically.

She disappeared for a while, then returned and laid next to me. She looked me in the eye and apologized for her response. "I don't like talking about my life. I already told you enough. When I told you about that old love story, it was just a moment of weakness," she said.

"What was? The fact that you told me or the story itself?" I asked.

She drew nearer. "Both things were weak."

How physically close she is. We could practically sleep touching one another if I stretched my arm by my side. Surprisingly, she took my arm herself, rested it under her head, and asked me if it was okay for her to sleep in that position. I agreed.

She closed her eyes and said, "I want to ask you something, and I hope you understand it well. I want you to forget the fact that I'm a woman and that you're a man. I just want us to deal with each other like two people in a shared disaster who could lean on one another without any feelings involved. I want to sleep close to you so I will feel safer, and not for any other purpose."

She proceeded to talk with her eyes still closed. "My relationships with the opposite sex, like yours, are complicated. That's why we're constantly arguing about different things. If we stay here for a long time, I want us to forget about our genders. I stopped myself from crying on your chest when I needed it the most, as I was extremely close to breaking down. Your possible masculine input scared me."

I put my hand on her face, opened her eyes with my thumb, and smiled. "That was my exact intention when I kissed you on the forehead. I did it because you saved me from breaking down. From the moment you cried on my chest after I almost drowned, I began to see you as a companion who's going through the same crisis as I am, not as a woman," I said.

She smiled and snuggled closer, almost nestling into me like a small child. I put my arm around her back and went to sleep.

I was awakened by the sunlight in the morning, and the following day was better. Calm weather, calm company, and tastier food, even though we still didn't eat meat because we couldn't find a heat source. We began to walk to the tunnel without discussing our impending decision: should we head to the shelter or remain outside? We were both leaning toward the idea of giving in. The possibility of spending an entire year in searching the island for a way out without any success was becoming more likely. Therefore, it was better to spend three years in a clean, safe place. In addition, if we could leave, where would we go? We were still captives, and they could still run experiments whether we liked it or not.

We slept the same way we did on the previous night, almost attached to each other—our new ritual. And just like the previous night, we woke up with our backs turned against each other. By noon, we reached the stream from which we drank on the first day, or so we thought. The water was so shallow that we could cross it near the headwaters. After that, we walked for a short distance on the riverbank, then wandered between the trees in the region that supposedly contained the entrance to the tunnel, but we couldn't find it anywhere.

We kept searching every inch of the area until we eventually gave up and began to discuss different possibilities. Was camouflaging the tunnel entrance a new part in the experiment, or had we simply lost track of the area? After all, neither of us had experienced walking in the woods... We sat down to rest for a while and began to eat some fruit. A bizarre howling noise, like the one we heard on our first day there, nearly deafened us.

The sound came nearer, the source obviously rushing toward us. We immediately dropped the fruits on the ground and ran in the direction of the river. I glimpsed a pack of wolves running behind us, but their movements were controlled, like the previous time. I considered climbing the nearest tree, but there wasn't a suitable one—all smooth trunks and no branches. We then continued running until we reached the riverbank. I asked Shadia if we should jump in the water. She responded, "Let's wait and see what they will do."

The wolves appeared through the trees, calmly walking. The pack of seven or eight wolves snarled and revealed their fangs as they neared. We cautiously retreated to avoid provoking them, getting in the water. The wolves continued to come closer as we continued to withdraw until the water reached their torsos and nearly our shoulders.

The situation remained calm, as if someone coached the wolves to surround us but not attack. I didn't doubt for a second that those wolves were trained, yet I didn't dare go near them or stop moving as they neared. We moved along the bank while still in deep water, following the river current. The wolves followed, neither chasing us or letting us be. A few minutes passed before the wolves decided to get out of the water, sit by the trees, and wait.

They watched carefully. If we tried to approach the bank, they got up and began to come close. If we walked parallel to the bank, they followed, maintaining an appropriate distance. Suddenly, Shadia let out several painful shrieks and jumped up in the water. I shifted my attention to her in fear, and soon understood what was happening firsthand when I felt numerous bites on my leg.

Startled, I moved away and pulled Shadia's hand so she would do the same. She resisted at first, but then tried to let herself float in the water. That didn't work, as we both continued to be bitten all over our legs. I felt a bite on my arm, so I extended my hand and caught my attacker. It was an inch-long lizard that resembled a crocodile, with sharp, fang-like teeth.

Instinctively and without discussing it, Shadia and I got out of the water and ran along the bank while the wolves chased us. I thought about turning around and facing them, because I was sure at that point that they wouldn't harm me. Shadia told me to wait before confronting them because we needed to have some sort of weapon to defend ourselves with. We went to the trees, where I picked out a thick branch and gave it to her, then took another for myself. We exchanged glances to encourage each other, then turned around to confront the wolves.

As the wolves approached we froze in fear, yet tried to intimidate them with the branches, waving them left and right in the air. The alpha of the pack snarled, drool dripping down its jaw.

"The drooling can only mean that the wolf is following its instinct only," Shadia said, almost in tears.

I cautiously walked toward it, swinging the branch at its face. It dodged and jumped at Shadia, who tried to step backward. She was imploring it not to hurt her, as though it understood what she was saying. Shortly thereafter, its fangs dug into her thigh. She shrieked and I screamed in rage, cursing while hitting it on the head with the branch as aggressively as I could.

The wolf let go of her thigh and turned to me at the same instant that two other wolves started to move as well. It glared at them while growling, as if ordering them to stay put. It then faced me, so I waved the branch around to scare it, but it moved astonishingly fast and grabbed the branch with its jaw. I tried to pull it away, but failed. The wolf grasped it strongly, taking it from my hand—almost tearing out my entire arm—then threw it with a quick head motion. It approached me, snarling, while drool dripped down its jaw much more than before.

19

Shadia was loudly wailing...in pain or distress, or perhaps both. I lay flat on the ground helplessly while the wolf hovered over me, sniffing my body before it ultimately ate me alive. In that exact moment, I wished I had resorted to the shelter from day one. After all, our resistance and attempts only went to waste and achieved nothing but a time filled with pain, fear, hunger, thirst, and the wasteful death of two Editians.

I failed to do what I saw people in movies do: scream at the wolf with my eyes wide open, challenging it to go ahead and kill me. I didn't shout at Shadia to close her eyes so she wouldn't witness my death. I was nothing but a hollow, humanly mass of panic, regret, and self-loathing. I blamed myself for the largest mistake in my life...after a series of multiple regrets.

The wolf raised its head to the sky and howled. With its large mouth open, it came at me, but suddenly a strong shiver moved from its body to mine. The wolf whimpered in pain and rolled over. My body still trembled, as if in the embrace of a strong electric current. I felt strong pain in my chest; my respiration was shallow and rapid. I struggled to take even one breath to fill my lungs.

Everything suddenly went dark.

When I woke up, Shadia's hands were on top of each other in the middle of my chest, pressing down with the strength of her body weight. Her face was covered in tears as she attempted a resuscitation in despair, muttering prayers. As soon as she noticed my open eyes, she grabbed my face firmly and thanked God while proceeding to cry even harder. She hugged me fiercely and continued to weep.

I didn't understand what was happening. I looked around me and noticed that all the wolves had vanished, except for the alpha one, which lay still.

Shadia said, "I'm now surer than ever that those wolves were trained, but it seems we provoked the alpha one enough to make it spiral out of control and execute its own plan. That's why our kidnappers killed it. They really intend to keep us alive."

There were holes in her pants in the center of her thigh that were covered in dry blood. I asked her how she was feeling.

"The pain is coming back now. I forgot all about it when I was trying to resuscitate you."

I wondered how she learned to perform that.

"A hospital nearby was giving a training course on how to perform CPR, so I attended out of curiosity," she said.

I almost jokingly asked if she performed the famous "the kiss of life" on me. But I decided not to say anything so I wouldn't upset her or push her away again.

I sat up and immediately felt dizzy. I crawled to the nearest tree with Shadia's help. We both leaned against its broad trunk. I let my head rest on her shoulder and she patted me, put her arm around me, and sympathetically held me closely. I asked again about her injury. *How are we going to dress it? Will she need one of those shots they give you after a dog's bite?*

It wasn't the only wound we acquired on that day—those small lizards also bit us several times. It was notable that none of our wounds ever became inflamed on the island. They even healed quickly with regard to the constant unsanitary state we lived in, in addition to the different water sources we swam in—be it the one in the tunnel, the river, or the sea.

It was almost nighttime as we rested near another stream. We got up to drink and pick fruit, struggling to move around. We approached the stream and Shadia suddenly exclaimed, "We're idiots! *This* stream is the one close to the tunnel opening, not the other one. Now we have to cross it and walk southeast."

I carefully considered the information and realized that she was probably right.

"Okay, we'll cross the stream and carry on with our search first thing in the morning," I said.

I was famished, but I was grossed out by all the fruit. I longed to hunt down and grill any creature that showed up, but we didn't get either a prey or fire. On that island, I went through different phases of ingratitude, always desiring something better. Just a second ago, it seemed, I only wished to remain alive. After surviving, I wanted to eat. After getting the chance to eat fruit, I was disgusted by the available options and coveted better food, then a better shelter, then my entire freedom.

Would freedom truly come last? Prisoners usually shouted for freedom at first, but after a period of despair, they asked for improved conditions. If their present conditions worsened, they longed to go back to the previous conditions that were initially unsatisfactory.

Was that our case on the island? Was it the purpose of the experiment? To explore humans' ability to endure and accept the unacceptable if the price was their basic safety? One Arab poet once said, "Don't quench my thirst with water of life and shame me about it, give me a bitter drink but respect my pride." I doubted he would say the same thing if he went through a situation similar to ours. It is easy to judge something you never experienced.

It was, however, a relief to know that my plan for when we woke up the following morning was to finally enter the shelter, where all our struggling would end. I shared these thoughts with Shadia, who listened without responding or discussing. After we finished picking fruit, she suggested we try lighting a fire like young boys did in camps—by using dry branches. She said that grilling the fruits over the fire might improve their flavor. I told her I never cared for camp activities or folkloric gullible nonsense.

She twisted her lips in disapproval and went to gather some dry branches, but soon groaned in pain, holding her injured thigh. She sat down once more with cold beads of sweat dotting her face. I asked her to get some rest and went to gather the branches myself, then brought them back to her. She picked one that was a foot long. She made sure it was dry, then she inserted the tip in the ground among dry leaves and smaller branches and kept twirling it rapidly between her hands, waiting for smoke to come out. It didn't work.

She threw the branch away in desperation and shrieked in anger, almost in tears. I approached her and patted her head, while her headscarf slid down to her upper neck. I promised her that everything was going to be okay.

"We've survived so many hardships, and it's all coming to an end now," I told her.

"But we didn't survive anything or beat anyone. We're just two rats in a maze, trying to make it in whichever path happens to be open," she said.

"Don't say that!" I said firmly. "We picked the harder path every single time. We challenged them. If we truly were maze rats, we would have accepted defeat from the very start."

My words to her were essentially a validation for myself, trying to justify my wrong decisions. Being on the island resembled the process of going through life: We were exposed to multiple choices. Sometimes we picked the easy way out; other times we chose to conquer the obstacles—depending on our strength, energy, and the scenario itself.

At that specific moment, I thought about the reason behind them picking the two of us specifically. Was it a mere chance? Were the Earthlings randomly chosen? And if that was the case, why were we—out of twenty million people living in the same city—the ones afflicted? Sometimes, having wolves or even a flood around was a blessing because they prevented us from thinking about such matters. We simply fought to survive.

I attempted to get up once more, but she tried to make me stay, so I assured her I was coming back soon. I brought back even harder and drier branches and asked her to try again. She picked one and began rotating it between her hands, then stopped as if she remembered something. She rotated it again, but in the opposite direction. Smoke finally appeared and a fire was ignited while we blew at it to increase its intensity. Our faces were so close to each other that they almost touched.

We grilled some fruits, which slightly improved their taste. I grabbed one of the larger branches and told her I was going to search for a prey to grill. "Just sit down and be thankful for once," she told me. I laughed, promising not to roam too far. I walked between the trees, trying to find a small animal or bird on any of the branches. I heard a scratchy noise behind one of the trees and found a crouched animal digging a hole in the ground. It looked like one of those large rats that attacked Shadia on our first day. It looked at me while its eyes shone in the dark, which made me hesitate to approach it.

Then I spotted four eyes shining in the dark, gazing at me. They belonged to two much smaller animals, and it became clear that it was a family, consisting of a mother and two pups. The mother suddenly jumped at me and scratched my leg, then retreated and attempted to attack once more, but I stepped back and felt guilty about wanting to kill her. She took this chance to escape with her two pups.

I examined the ground where she was digging and found another hole with a big rabbit making room for itself. I was able to catch it, then returned to Shadia, exciting myself with the idea of a delicious dinner.

20

Zahra was supposed to arrive at the hospital at four in the afternoon. Omar requested that his doctors dress his wounds early that day so he could have more time to prepare to meet her. He sent someone to buy him an expensive perfume bottle, which he later sprayed on the gauze covering his body and on the body parts that were exposed. He asked the hospital's barber to neatly trim his hair, shave his beard, and apply a scented aftershave. Surely Omar didn't forget to give him a generous tip. He gave one of the hospital janitors another generous tip as well to clean his room and bring in new sheets, as if he were preparing to host her in his own house.

He felt happy and thrilled, completely forgetting what was going on in his life, including the burns and physical pain. For the first time since he was admitted to the hospital, he didn't mind sitting in the whirlpool bath. He didn't even complain about his dressing and quietly endured the pain. Luckily for him, Dr. Hend, who was more tender and gentler, was in charge that day. At exactly 3 p.m., one hour before Zahra's arrival, one of the nurses came into his room with a blood bag, intending to hang it on the IV pole and connect it to his neck. He asked her to postpone it to a later time, to which she refused. He raised his voice and strongly objected, claiming that if she hung the blood bag and connected it to his neck, he was going disconnect it and let it spill all over the floor. He feared that if the blood raised his body temperature, then fever would take over his body and brain, meaning he couldn't converse with Zahra. Dr. Hend wanted to know why he refused.

"Dr. Zahra is coming in an hour to inject me with her numbing medication. I'm afraid that if my temperature goes up, the session will be postponed to a later day."

Dr. Hend didn't protest and listened to his wishes. She told the nurse to keep the bag in the blood bank and bring it out after Dr. Zahra left.

The day before, the department chief had inquired about the price of the electronic tablets that Omar earlier bought for the two young boys. When Omar told him, the man was shocked by the high cost, blaming him for being frivolous.

"You could have spent that money on medications, or equipment for our operating rooms instead. Next time, don't buy anything before checking with me." He then asked Omar who gave him the idea to buy the tablets, but he feared that the doctor might get blamed or penalized for it, so he said, "No one in particular."

Before leaving the room, the chief changed his tone into a friendlier one and said, "The foreign expert surgeon will pass by in a few days, and he will check your case."

The hour passed tremendously slowly. Omar kept picturing the moment they would meet. Was it going to be a regular doctor-patient visit, or did she feel anything different toward him after the previous visit? He noticed her nervousness when he touched her hand with his fingertips, and he observed her submission to his request to read his novel. Would she really read it, or did she simply take the USB from him to shut him down politely?

He secretly prayed that no emergency patient would show up at the last moment and share his room, or that no patient in a different ward would get worse, hence moving them to his intensive care unit room. He wondered if the air conditioner was too cold, so he asked one of the nurses to turn it down.

"But you usually like it cold!" the nurse said. He didn't respond and tell her that he knew Zahra didn't like cold rooms.

It was past four and she still hadn't shown up. Five minutes passed, then ten. He was gasping for air and his heart began to race. His heart already beat too fast due to his condition, so it wouldn't handle beating a second faster.

Zahra finally showed up at the door, looking like a princess out of a fairytale. She wore an ankle-length dress, a close-fitting shirt that covered her arms, a rosy headscarf, and short heels. The bright smile on her face had a refreshing effect, similar to that of cold water after a long hot day. Her ruddy, tanned complexion took over your senses, the way aged wine did. Zahra's wide, brown eyes were capable of soothing your nerves, overwhelming you with peaceful energy, like how you felt after an intimate prayer on a silent night.

She casually reached out her hand to shake his, asking if he was ready for the session.

"Yes, but we have to wait for Dr. Hend to bring the syringes."

"She doesn't need to come. I can get started without her."

Omar, however, begged Zahra to wait, claiming that he would feel safer if she was around. His request seemed to surprise her, but he saw she understood it better when she learned that Dr. Hend was in the operating room and was going to be thirty minutes late.

She smiled. "Okay, I will sacrifice thirty minutes of my time just for you because you're a good person, and because I like what I've read so far in the book."

"You like Nescafé coffee, don't you?" He claimed his relative learned that from her secretary and mentioned it to him.

"I'll drink some coffee when I get back to my house after we're done. How did you feel after your last session?"

"I can never thank you enough!" he said gratefully and appreciatively wished her happiness and comfort. He assumed most of her patients said that. They were soon interrupted when one of the workers brought in a cup of Nescafé coffee and a small table.

"I'm like a rich prisoner around here," Omar said. "The guards and fellow prisoners do anything I tell them to. As for the janitors, I pay them small tips. I don't pay other patients' relatives, though. They help me out of the kindness of their hearts, without even waiting for a thank you."

"Egyptians are always there for each other," she said while slowly sipping her coffee.

"Sympathizing with someone other than yourself doesn't require you to be Egyptian," he said. "You only have to be human. Compassion and empathy don't belong to solely one race." He continued to recount many stories about people who helped strangers in need for utterly no reason at all except humanity.

He talked while contemplating her face, noticing the eyeliner on the corner of her eyelids and the simple red tint on her lips and cheeks. *She didn't have any makeup on the last time I saw her.*

***

Omar looked at her in a way that made her feel shy, so she excused herself, saying that she would return shortly. She went to the doctors' office and entered the bathroom inside, closing the door after her. She stood in front of the mirror, catching her breath. *What is going on? Why did I dress up for him, and why do I feel so ecstatic the more he eats me up with his eyes?* She felt like a thrilled and joyful teenager delightfully entering a trap of unidentified feelings.

She'd read a couple of chapters from his book and got the impression he was prejudiced against women. The protagonist of the novel generally took a firm stand against women, and she felt that the protagonist and the author possessed things in common. But that didn't make sense, because what she was experiencing with the author was completely different. For instance, he was going through the most challenging and painful experience anyone could go through, with the atrocious injuries he suffered from, yet he made sure that the janitor cleaned his room and prepared the right coffee just for her.

Who is this man? Why does he behave this way? He arranges his room and his bed, and makes sure an expensive-smelling perfume takes over the air, as if he were preparing to host his girlfriend.

She decided to wait in the office until Dr. Hend joined them, sitting on the leather couch next to the desk and stressfully cracking her knuckles. She eventually got up—after having taken a long, deep breath—and headed to the room once again. She sat next to him, took another sip of coffee, and asked him about the cause of his burns.

"It doesn't really matter how I got them. What matters is how I will be treated from them, even though I've lost hope. That's why I don't care much for the how and when."

His response made her heart sink. "Despair isn't appropriate in your case. Plus, I asked about your chances for healing well and learned that they are quite good."

He lit up and asked, with a beaming face, "When did you ask about my case?"

"It's normal for a doctor to check on the patient they are treating and learn everything about their case."

His smile almost faded from his face after she referred to him in a distant, practical manner, as a patient. Then she added, "And don't forget, you're an important patient. You're a writer and your fans need you."

He laughed, telling her she could count the number of his fans on one hand, and that it was his honor that she joined them.

She wanted to get a better understanding of his vivid imagination in the story, and he told her it was based on a true story: one that explained how he ended up in that hospital bed. She asked about the protagonist and his prejudice against Shadia and women in general, wondering why he wrote about a protagonist with such misogynistic beliefs. After all, Omar specifically asked for a female doctor to perform this extremely complicated and dangerous procedure.

He answered her all questions, impressing her with his knowledge and way of presenting his arguments. She asked why he chose to work as a technician and didn't use his certificate to search for a job instead.

He answered, "You don't ask a question like that in Egypt. A certificate these days is nothing but decoration or a societal ornament; it just allows you to marry a woman with a college certificate while feeling good about yourself."

He mentioned how he went to work in Abu Dhabi but was exposed to fraud, losing a large amount of money in the process. After he returned, he'd decided to overcome that obstacle by buying a small plumbing store with reasonable expenses. It brought him customers who asked for plumbing services, in addition to buying tools from him. He hadn't, however, abandoned his love for writing, but he spent more on this hobby than what he gained from the plumbing store's profits.

Hend entered the room, warmly welcoming Zahra and repeatedly apologizing for being late. "I'm so glad Omar introduced you to me. Thanks to you, I learned a new procedure of curing pain that I didn't know much about before," she said.

In less than a minute, everything was prepared and Zahra began to do her job. She put disinfectant on his back, applied local anesthesia, and inserted the thick needle in his body, asking if he felt an electric sensation running in his leg. After confirming the location, she began to inject the carefully prepared formula to numb his pain.

The pain vanished from his thigh and his other leg, which meant only his arms were left. Zahra wanted to inject the nerves at the root of his neck, above his clavicles. To do that, she needed an ultrasound device. Hend seemed anxious to learn that technique, so she said she was going to look for one and bring it as fast as possible. Omar suggested they postpone it to another visit, but Hend refused and insisted she would bring the device any way she could because she was eager to watch the procedure.

When they were left alone, Zahra and Omar remained quiet for some time. Omar then initiated the conversation, mentioning the expert who was going to visit Egypt in a week, who might visit the hospital and check on his case.

Zahra's face lit up. "I'm happy to hear that! I am sure he will have viable options for your case."

Omar then asked her how her work was going, followed by a cautious question about her personal life at home...specifically if anyone waited there. She answered in a different tone, briefly and firmly.

After that, he immediately changed the subject. "I can't wait for your next visit so you can tell me what you think of the book."

"I might not visit anymore. My job is done as soon as I inject the nerves affecting your arms," she said.

"Hold off on it then!" he said. She responded that his case couldn't handle any postponement. "Well, can't you visit a poor patient only because you feel sorry for him?"

He asked it as a joke, but she glowered. "Mr. Omar, I don't think it's appropriate for me to visit you unless it has to do with your condition. Other than that, there's no reason."

He choked on his words and felt suffocated by tears, so he kept quiet. The following minute passed as slowly as a year, until Hend eventually returned, looking disappointed.

"I didn't find the device anywhere." She said to Dr. Zahra, "Can you visit on another day and time that matches with my shift? I really want to witness the procedure."

Additionally, she asked if Zahra would agree to be her master's thesis supervisor. Dr. Hend said she intended to suggest to her professor that she write her thesis on treating burn patients using Zahra's method. Zahra welcomed the idea and showed excitement in supervising her.

Hend excused herself to go back to work and Zahra was left again with Omar. She explained to him what she was going to do the next time she visited him. "I will come in two days, and that will be the last session."

He thanked her, with tears running down his cheeks despite himself. "I'm sorry if I spoke with too much familiarity."

Her heart broke when she saw his tears, almost making her teary as well. She secretly blamed herself for her rough way of speaking to him.

"No, I'm sorry. I didn't mean to offend you," she said, while shaking his hand. She found herself promising that she would keep herself updated on his case even after she finished her injections.

21

Three whole years of our lives was the price we were going to pay if we chose the safety of the shelter over the chaos of the island. Our informant hadn't clarified what was going to happen after we finished our imprisonment period. I even contemplated whether the notion of "three years" was just part of the experiment. Maybe they wanted to study our ability to reach a choice, and after we pressed the button, a lamp here or there would light up and we would hear a voice: "The first part of the experiment is over. On to the next."

I woke up before Shadia did. She was still sleeping in my arms, different from the usual. Her thick silky hair covered her face, went down to her shoulders, and extended onto my chest, like a connecting bridge. Before coming to the island, I never imagined sleeping next to someone who invaded my personal space so closely and let the weight of her head rest on my arm. Shadia, the island, or the experiment itself managed to achieve that. Regardless of who or what it was, it opened a window in my soul that allowed my body to accept sleeping next to someone almost attached to me.

I moved the hair from her face and gazed at her. She opened her eyes. "Good morning!" she said in an uncharacteristically soft voice. I contemplated her face and mused about the strange chance that brought us this close together. She smiled when she noticed me staring and timidly asked for the reason. I myself didn't know, which made me change the subject. "How's your injury now?"

"I feel fine," she said.

Our plan was simply to cross the stream, search for the door to the tunnel, then press on the button—simple and clear. When I suggested we eat first, she scolded me in her usual manner. "All you care about is eating! The shelter will have food, probably much better than those tasteless fruits." Then she asked if I was fairly certain about our decision.

"I don't see the point in resisting them. I honestly think the whole 'three years' promise is part of their plan. They're probably testing our ability to challenge them," I said.

She agreed. "We didn't give up easily so far, but it feels stupid to keep going in a losing battle... But I still don't get why they brought me here if they wanted to experiment on males?"

I jokingly said, "Maybe they want to test my ability to handle moody females."

She lightly nudged my shoulder, laughing flirtatiously for the first time since we met. Even on our calmest days, we hadn't felt that much at peace. Our walls were beginning to crumble, allowing a burgeoning closeness. From the first day I met her, I thought that she was prejudiced against men, the same way I was against women, but for different reasons. The common result, however, was our avoidance of the opposite sex.

When she began to rise, I noticed she was trying to conceal her physical pain. I asked her about it, but she insisted it was nothing. We quietly walked until we reached the stream, hurriedly crossing it so that the bloodsucking leeches wouldn't fasten on like they did before.

When we reached our destination and Shadia attempted to step up from the stream, raising her leg, she shrieked in pain. I was instantly concerned and asked her to rest, but she insisted we carry on. We walked less than three meters until she screamed again, grabbing me before falling to the ground.

I asked to take a look at her wounds, to which she agreed in pain. She asked, however, that I not touch it. I explored the bite marks of the wolf, and it seemed that he'd dug his fangs deeply into her flesh. The wounds reeked of a bloody liquid, while the skin around the area was red. I asked her if she could carry on walking after we rested for a bit, and she nodded. She leaned her back against a tree trunk, but was too drained, so I let her lie down on the ground and use my lap as a pillow.

"Maybe the reason they brought you here is to test my ability to carry you!" I said. I was thinking to myself whether it was better to head to the spot where we left our bags and search for a shot to give her, or an ointment to help her with the pain, or should we both go to the tunnel and use whatever we needed there instead.

We spent a long time chatting and laughing, worrying about nothing else—or at least pretending not to. I asked her to try walking while leaning on me, so she grabbed onto my arm and put her weight on her good thigh until she was able to get up. The moment she began walking, however, she groaned and almost fell to the ground again. That time I managed to catch her and slowly sit her down. It wasn't possible at that point to walk in the woods because of her condition, especially since we'd forgotten where the entry to the tunnel was.

I decided to leave her and go fetch our bags, even though I wasn't sure I was going to find them. The distance was at least six kilometers overall, which meant it would take at least an hour if I walked as rapidly as I could. She looked scared and asked me not to leave her alone.

"It won't take long! And I promise, no matter what I may encounter on my way, it won't stop me from coming back to you as fast as I can."

I headed to the riverbank and sprinted alongside until I ran out of breath, so I slowed my pace and eventually jogged. I glimpsed our tent from afar, so I moved quickly once more until I finally reached it. I didn't, however, find any trace of the bags. They seemed to have vanished into thin air. I looked everywhere around the tent. I searched along the riverbank, then hunted at the bottom of the tree that we tried to cut down, but found absolutely nothing, not even the small axe we used.

I took the tent with me, as I considered using it as a stretcher to move Shadia, possibly dragging her to the tunnel door. I walked back hurriedly, also by the riverbank. I counted the streams I passed by so I wouldn't get lost. I finally reached her, only to find her hands covering her face in pain. When she heard the sound of my steps, she raised her face and looked at me with teary eyes.

"Why are you crying?" I asked, sitting down and holding her.

"The pain in my thigh isn't bearable anymore and I was terrified they were going to do something to you, using one of their tricks."

I patted her back and reassured her, kissing her on the forehead. I took a deep breath. "It's okay. This will all be over soon."

I put down the tent and told her to slowly crawl to it using her arms. She started to move, but soon groaned again and stopped while tears slid down her face. She asked me to hold her to calm her down, so I sat next to her and she rested her head on my chest. At that moment, I had an overwhelming desire to burst into tears myself, without knowing the reason why. I let my tears go, which she apparently felt, because she raised her head and examined my face.

We silently looked at each other while tears covered both of our faces. If whoever in charge was watching at that moment, they probably wouldn't understand what was going on. I rested my hand on her cheek, looked around, then looked at her again, whispering that I was never going to leave her. We got even closer, and she extended her arms and surrounded my back with them, laying her head on my shoulder.

After a long time, she finally settled on top of the tent and was ready to be moved. I grabbed two edges of the tent and started dragging her slowly for two or three meters.

She eventually suggested, "I think it's better if you look for the door tunnel first, then drag me to it."

She made a valid point, so I dragged her to the nearest tree and sat her there.

It was a fruity tree we were both familiar with. I picked two fruits and gulped them down before going on my search journey. I spotted a group of monkeys gathered on some high trees nearby; they were alertly watching us. Suddenly they started to throw hard fruit, which felt like rocks, at both of us. I protected Shadia by covering her with my back turned to them, thinking I'd wait until they finished, but they kept throwing more and more fruit. I gripped the tent's edges and began dragging Shadia in a different direction, and they stopped. I sat down to catch my breath and they went back to throwing fruit. When I got up and moved again, they stopped.

It was strange! Whenever I stopped, they threw fruit, and when I moved, they stopped, as if forcing me to keep going. I walked in a straight line in hopes of miraculously finding the entrance in front of me. Few meters later, however, I found a different group of monkeys throwing fruit at us. We were being targeted from both directions, and neither group stopped until I turned right. At first it seemed that they were simply teasing, even though the last thing I needed at the time was a group of bored monkeys who threw annoying fruit.

Eventually we found the entry to the tunnel in front of us, ajar like I last left it. I opened the door as far as I could, cautiously dragged Shadia in her tent, and asked her to use her good leg to climb down the ladder. She was eventually able to do it—after plenty of shrieks and groans, which I found more painful than anything else we'd went through. I descended the ladder by her side until I reached the ground, then raised my arms to catch her and let her down carefully as well.

We both sat to catch our breath, and I was ready to go press the button when she surprisingly asked, "You don't think the monkeys were directing us to the tunnel in a way, do you?"

I opened my mouth in disbelief. How did I miss that? They truly were guiding us.

Are our kidnappers in that much of a hurry, or is this the last part of the experiment? Was the wolf meant to bite Shadia so violently that I can't find any other solution but to go to the tunnel? Why do they insist that we give up, and what will it cost them if we refuse to enter? Isn't the experiment essentially to study our capacity to endure?

Maybe those who supposedly died for our sakes were only part of the experiment as well. Perhaps they didn't truly die, and our captors only wanted us to think that they did. Their sole purpose could be to make us weaker and convince us to submit, then wait until imaginary "help" arrived. Maybe it wasn't our endurance they wanted to study, but our submission: what it would take for us to submit. Shadia was suffering, and the bite might have been poisonous or unsanitary.

She requires treatment. And to do that, I must press that button.

What would that make me other than a bull that they used for insemination then got rid of? Even if they decided to keep me alive, I would be nothing but a useless semen bag.

What if I refuse to submit and make them keep trying? Will they treat me differently, or will they kill and abandon me?

Whatever the givens or the purpose of the experiment were, the only thing I knew was that Shadia was about to die and I had no other option but save her life by giving up. If it was my own life, I would have the privilege to reconsider my choice, but I couldn't do the same with her life. I didn't even want to consult her first before deciding. I headed to the button, ready to press it, but an idea popped in my head right before doing it.

What if I take it off the wall and connect the wires that open the door to the tunnel—after disconnecting any wires that might close the door? Of course, they will watch me do it, probably capture us, and end the experiment once and for all.

Perhaps they were going to let us live for a couple of more days. Whatever their decision was going to be, if I executed my plan, I would ruin their game and rebel against them. I asked Shadia for her opinion. She agreed with me but asked, "Are you good with electrical work?"

I stuttered before saying my answer: "I worked as apprentice in an electrical supply store during middle school, and I was mostly bad at it. The storeowner kicked me out after two months."

She smiled at me. "I trust you. Nothing bad will happen, even if you connect the wrong cables. The point is, we're not going to play by their rules anymore."

I inserted a knife between the button and the wall, struggling to take it off. I eventually managed to, and found many intermingling wires: all seven led to a tube in the wall. I cautiously disconnected them one by one and began to try different linkage combinations until I eventually found the right ones.

22

Yes, the task was fraught with danger, but the kind of risks that resembled moving a chess piece suddenly. The worst-case scenario was losing the game, but on that day, my game didn't even have a losing or winning point. My move wasn't going to create an unexpected result—it was nothing but a mere statement. A disapproval. An unproductive protest. A sarcastic Facebook post or a video with a comical voiceover.

All the cables resembled one another, as if whoever designed them intended to make getting involved with them extra challenging. I always despised electricity and connecting wires together. Whenever someone mentioned anything about it, I remembered the electric shocks I received from the storeowner who persisted in trying to teach me what I couldn't comprehend.

I attempted to connect two wires together, the first with the second, then the third. I didn't get any response, and didn't hear any sound except for Shadia's muffled groans, which made me feel utterly helpless.

I reexamined the wires one by one. I eventually discovered that one of the wires was different in terms of where it extended from the tube. It was singular and central to the rest of the wires: there were two on its right, two on its left, and two underneath it. Each two were attached at their outlet, and only that wire was by itself in the center.

I connected the central wire to the two on its right and noticed a subtle spark emitting due to the coupling, but nothing happened. Moments later, I heard a burbling sound coming from the opposite direction, and water started to flow toward us. I quickly disconnected the wires, because their linkage was apparently the reason behind what just happened. In no time, the water stopped flowing.

I then connected the central wire to the two on its left, and another spark was emitted. I expected another trap, but I heard a whirring sound emitted near the entrance of the tunnel. The door began to slowly open, revealing a large hall that contained several wardrobes, a couch, fluffy chairs, a dining table, and three doors. I exultantly screamed and jumped up and down. I was exalted with what we'd achieved. I kneeled and hugged Shadia, and she reciprocated while she wiggled with joy.

I slowly helped her move until we reached the shelter. The sparkling floor was immediately stained by the dirt stuck to her clothes. I carried her and carefully sat her down at the couch, then I took a look inside the wardrobes, looking for one that contained medical supplies.

I found a cupboard that contained folded clothes, which I temporarily kept in their place, another one with tools, and a third that contained medications, salves, and injections. I examined them and discovered that most of them sported Arabic names, making it seem like everything they brought was perfectly suited for our stay. I took one of the ointments that was labeled "wound cream" and a painkiller injection, and headed to Shadia. I sat on the floor in front of the couch on which I laid her. I spread some of the ointment on the wound through the hole in her pants.

"Go look for scissors, please!" she said. When I asked her why, she impatiently said, "Just go get them."

I brought them to her from the tools wardrobe. She cut her pant leg off, revealing the entire wound. I'd wanted to do the same thing, but was hesitant. She was more rational and realized that there was no reason to be awkward about it.

She took some of the ointment. "It's better for me to apply it—your hands aren't that gentle," she said with a tired smile. She spread it over the wound until it was completely covered and then put her head back, pursing her lips and moaning in pain.

I wanted to give her the injection on her shoulder, the site that was indicated on the cover photo. Her shirt, however, had long sleeves that prohibited the injection. She pointed at the scissors and I knew what to do. I cut the sleeve and sank the syringe into her shoulder, anticipating its effect, and I didn't have to wait long. The pain immediately decreased—perhaps even vanished. She said, "I previously assumed that our captors were more advanced than us, but it appears that their medicine is almost the same."

I didn't respond to her. My head was preoccupied with what awaited us, so I said, "They must have already seen us, and they are probably preparing a new hindrance."

I wondered if they closed the tunnel door on us. I hurriedly got up, crossed the shelter's door, climbed the ladder, and saw that the door was still open. I went back to her and again mentioned our next steps and the upcoming disaster that probably awaited us.

She interrupted me by putting her hand on my mouth. "Can we just enjoy this moment of peace, quiet, and cleanness?"

I stopped talking, but I was surprised at her behavior. Women didn't usually react that way; in my experience, they usually preempted a disaster before it happened and assumed that any surprise hid endless tribulations. I told her I was going to check what was behind the doors. She nodded and closed her eyes, preparing to fall asleep.

Three doors: I opened the first door using a button on its right. It slid horizontally, revealing a long corridor. The wall on the right contained many shelves that held various cans of different shapes and sizes. The left wall included an opening that led to a side room without a door. Many glass-doored booths that looked like vending machines extended along the corridor, which was almost twenty meters long. I entered the side room, which turned out to be a kitchen with a stove, two sinks, cupboards, and two small tables, one of which was wheeled.

I returned to the main hall to see if Shadia was asleep. She was, so I went back to the kitchen, picked out some of the cans, and emptied them onto plates. I removed two juice glasses, filled a flask with water, and put everything on the wheeled table. I rolled it to the main room and put it next to the couch.

I gently patted Shadia on the shoulder and whispered her name. She awakened, sat up, and claimed she wasn't in pain anymore. Her face lit up when she saw the food, and we both devoured it in a matter of seconds, even though it tasted strange. After we finished, we got up to explore what was behind the other two doors. Each one led to a small bedroom with a large bathroom that contained a big bathtub. The bathrooms included towels and varying clothes to demonstrate which room was whose.

We entered our separate rooms to finally change our worn-out clothes and take a shower. I stood under the showerhead, washing away all the dirt, filth, mud, and the tree and grass remains stuck in my hair and all over my body. I dried my body under a specifically made hot-air dryer, whose use was demonstrated via pictures. The boxers were made out of a material that resembled medical gloves, but they were comfy and light on the skin. Then I put on silky-yet-stretchy shirts and trousers. They easily expanded as I dressed and they fit perfectly.

When I came out of the room, Shadia was still in hers. I waited on a fluffy chair, humming a song by Iman Al Bahr Darwish.[21] I didn't know what reminded me of it, but as I hummed, I was thinking that maybe I wasn't so unlucky after all. Shadia was a companion who improved my defective ideas and

---

[21] Iman Al Bahr Darwish (in Arabic ايمان البحر درويش): A famous Egyptian singer; grandson of singer and composer Sayed Darwish.

helped me make more rational decisions. I handled her flaws, even though I couldn't do that with any woman before her—not even the ones I married. We shared very short yet passionate moments: several touches that enlightened my soul, brief teary hugs that healed my wounds, and a kiss that lasted less than a second but affected me in a way that previous longer kisses never did.

She opened her bedroom door and came out wearing a close-fitting shirt and tight pants that gave her an attractive look—like a superhero in one of those sci-fi movies, who wore leather suits that complimented their bodies. Her hair was uncovered and still somewhat wet.

When she saw me, she shyly said, "The outfit is embarrassing!"

"Never mind it. How's your wound?"

"I put more ointment on it and the pain is almost gone. Maybe their medicine is better than ours after all."

I stood up and approached her, feeling a strong need to hold her. She said, "Whatever happens, I will accept it as long as we're doing it together. You are my hero and my knight in shining armor. In a way, you healed my soul." She spoke words that I wanted to say. She uttered everything I'd reflected on while waiting for her to come out of her room.

I embraced her without any fear or hesitance, and she hugged me back without holding back, and it didn't seem as if she felt guilty. It lasted for a long, long time.

"You can sit down if you're in pain," I said.

"Even if I stood like this for ten more hours, I don't think I will feel the pain."

We both were entranced by the moment of transcendence, a long moment that allowed both our souls and hearts to touch each other while our breathing synced. Then our lips touched.

I'm not sure whether I kissed her first or she kissed me, but I remember she was close-eyed, trembling, eager, and yearning. Her full, luscious lips melted smoothly into mine. She would pull back, open her eyes, and inspect my face, as if reassuring herself that she wasn't dreaming, then she'd get close again for another round of fervent kisses. I was captivated and shared her passion and longing, while trying to make sure I wasn't hallucinating like the crazy writer I was. Her hands were also adding to our kisses, as though her lips wanted to take over. Her hands stroked my face, moved on my neck and back, then rested on my chest at the same moment that she pulled her face back to stare at mine with infatuation. After five rounds of consecutive kisses followed by intimate stares, we both dissolved into a long, tight embrace, interrupted by frequent shivers that were either mine or hers.

It was a once in a lifetime moment, and that's why it didn't last for long. We were still standing when we smelled a strong odor coming from the direction of the tunnel. I raced out to understand what was happening and saw a cloud of smoke moving from the end of the tunnel. I assumed that was the source of the odor, so I attempted to close the door of the shelter. Shadia screamed at me not to because it might not open again. I didn't listen to her that time. I resolutely pulled the door, but it didn't move beyond a few centimeters.

I ran toward her, took her by the hand, and opened the door leading to my room. I closed it after we'd entered, and we both sat on my bed, waiting. A few minutes passed and nothing happened, so we thought we were safe. I was about to suggest that I look outside to see what was happening. Before I could speak, we were taken aback by the door to my room—it opened as wide as it could, then gas entered the space all at once, filling our noses and eyes. We tried to hold our breath, but to no avail. Everything eventually went dark.

23

By the time Zahra turned fifteen, she began to look like a beautiful young lady. Her femininity was complete in a way that made her appear ready to perfectly fit in a wedding dress. When attending a private lesson at her teacher's house, Mrs. Amal, she was obviously the most mature and feminine out of the two other girls who joined her. One time, the teacher's husband interrupted the lesson and asked his wife to go calm their fussy, crying baby. As soon as Mrs. Amal left them, the husband smiled at the girls and advised them to study hard for school. Then he put his hand on Zahra and specifically directed his advice toward her.

It didn't feel like a harmless touch. It was a stroke that moved from her upper to lower back. He squeezed her flesh, evaluating her curviness. Her face went sullen and she didn't speak.

She didn't understand a word during the rest of the lesson. Zahra was scared to tell her mother so she wouldn't accuse her of being in the wrong. Two whole days passed, during which she felt like a crucified slave getting their head eaten by wild birds. She decided to confess what happened to her grandmother, who in return told her a saying that stuck with her forever: "The fear of saying NO is the worst thing you can submit to. It brings poverty to men, and brings shame to women."

Ever since that day, she considered fear to be her worst enemy. It only resulted in shame, especially when it came to dealing with men. Her grandmother told her that the movie *The Nightingale's Prayer*[22] was a clear example of that. The character Hanady lost her life because of a fear to say no, not because of love—because her sister Amna loved the same man, but she was strong enough to say no.

When Zahra turned Omar down, it was nothing but a natural reaction from a woman who despised fear, especially in dealing with men. That time, however, she felt like she went overboard. The man truly did love her—his tears were only an indication of his deep affection. They weren't a result of wounded pride or dignity; they exposed the true feelings of a heartbroken man. At that time she felt his love even more strongly than before. He loved her without limits, without calculations, and without expectations.

The first person she fell in love was with a fellow in college. In her third year of study, he kept trying to get closer to her, and despite everyone's warnings, she eventually fell in love with him. He didn't do well at school, he smoked, and he was seen with many different girls. She told him that to be with her, he must work harder and commit to no one but her. For two years, they became the most hard-

---

[22] *The Nightingale's Prayer* (in Arabic دعاء الكروان): A 1959 Egyptian movie. Hanady, a maid, is killed by her uncle because she got pregnant by her master. Her sister Amna tries to avenge her by killing the master. Despite trying to resist his seduction, she falls in love with him instead.

working students in their class and were perceived as the perfect loved birds. He told her he was going to ask her for hand in marriage after the exams of their final semester.

Shortly before their exams, Zahra realized that he was secretly dating another girl who constantly met him at his apartment. Her experience with him made Zahra walk away from love and never look back, and she decided to marry through an arranged marriage.

She refused many suitors after that experience. Each one held his own set of unrealistic conditions, as if they were doing her a favor by choosing her to be their wife. One suitor ordered her to choose an easy medical specialty that would accommodate her wifely duties, another told her how to spend her own salary, and another would only agree to marry if she traveled with him to work in a country in the Gulf—and he demanded half her salary.

She was eventually engaged to an open-minded engineer who worked at a prestigious company. He told he was honored to marry someone who did what she did, and that her constant promotions at work would reflect well on their future children's upbringing. He was sweet, generous, and understanding: a dream come true. After her father's passing, however, his attitude changed, especially when she asked him to let her sick mother come and live with them. He completely rejected the idea, and during a heated discussion, he uttered hurtful words that revealed his true colors and crystallized to Zahra how everything he had said before was nothing but a bunch of made-up lies.

She never met a man who offered her what she was looking for. She wasn't the dreamy type who was invested in a love affair or romantic fantasies; she simply wanted to meet an understanding, loyal, and reliable man. It seemed to her that the kind she was looking for was extinct.

Omar didn't offer her anything except for a pure, genuine love—one that was new to her. She didn't know that type of love existed, but it was still a fantastic love that wasn't going anywhere. Like the hunchback's love for Esmeralda,[23] Omar perceived her in a way that no other person did. Unfortunately, his love wasn't going to result in anything, whether he lived or died.

A while back, Zahra was expecting a visit from Moushira, her best friend. They remained close despite the large distance between them. Moushira was the only person in her class who experienced a successful love story—with Mahmoud. The two got married after graduating and traveled after getting their master's degree. Moushira visited Zahra every year during summer vacation, when the two managed to catch up on each other's stories and gossip. It was only on her most recent visit that Moushira didn't bring her kids to Zahra's house, perhaps after learning that Zahra's mother's condition became worse after amputating her leg.

Zahra's room looked the exact same way it did during their college years, and it remained Moushira's favorite place to hang out since they

---

[23] A reference to *The Hunchback of Notre Dame*, a French novel by Victor Hugo published in 1831.

used to study there. One of them sat on the bed, and the other sat on the couch. Moushira's method of study was to speak in different voice levels to repeat and memorize the material, but Zahra preferred visual learning.

On her last visit, Moushira opened up and complained about her husband Mahmoud, claiming he had become a different person. He was thinking about taking a second wife, reminding her that it was allowed by God. With a sense of virtue and protection, he told her that he was going to offer marriage another woman who needed the support of a husband. A fifteen-year-old love story was going to end with the involvement of a new woman. It started out as a joke between them, then he began to discuss it more seriously, even claiming that it might bring back the old fire to their marriage if a new addition arrived.

Zahra knew how proud her friend was—she wouldn't normally talk about such a sensitive subject unless she had reached the end of her rope. "I don't remember the last time we were intimate. When we traveled to Saudi Arabia, that closeness was gone."

Zahra offered her some homemade cakes. "A new place has nothing to do with intimacy. It has to do with the passing of time, and of course the person you're with," she said.

She reminded Moushira of their other friend who used to sometimes join in their studies. That young lady married a much older doctor and traveled with him right after she was done with her internship. Her marriage was worse than Moushira's, because whereas Mahmoud handled having kids, the other man was only there physically.

Moushira let out laugh. "And he wasn't even that physical! She complained once about it. At least you experienced lovemaking—I've been missing that for fourteen years."

What Zahra admired the most about Moushira was that she never dealt with Zahra the way her other friends did. They usually treated her with pity, reminding her of how much her life was missing without a husband, and that it was necessary make some sacrifices to get one. Some were even scared of being envied by her, so they excessively complained to her about their lives, and even hid their children. Moushira, however, loved her in a way that was free of jealousy, envy, or competitiveness.

Serving Moushira a plate of om ali,[24] Zahra abruptly said, "I have an interesting story for you."

"You're going to ruin my diet, but go ahead!" Moushira said, accepting the plate.

Zahra then proceeded to recount her story with Omar, starting from his relative's visit to her clinic all the way to him tearing up and apologizing to her after she turned him down. She mentioned how much she felt he knew her well, that he genuinely cared for her, and that she was conflicted about his overwhelming feelings of love.

She mentioned how he deliberately cut their first session short so he could see her again, even though he would have to endure additional pain, and how

---

[24] Om ali (in Arabic ام علي): A traditional Egyptian dessert made of pastry, sugar, raisins, and milk.

he practically begged her to wait and come for another session so he could meet and talk to her. She spoke about her impression of his book, and how his protagonist's developing relationship with the heroine was starting to make her jealous, even though it was a work of fiction.

"Lucky you!" said Moushira.

Zahra scolded her. "This isn't a good time for one of your jokes!"

But Moushira insisted that the story truly did make her heart race from the way she spoke about him, and that their bond was unprecedented to her. That's why she considered Zahra lucky for experiencing such a wonderful feeling, even it was just once.

Zahra contemplated her friend's words. *Is it true, or does it come from Moushira's frustration with her own love life? Should I give into my feelings and let go of my pride? How will people perceive me if I visit him after I'm done with his treatment?*

If she let go, she would also have to stop thinking about how she'd feel if something unfortunate happened to him, like his dying, for instance. She needed to consider what would happen if he lived a healthy life, or if he lived with physical or emotional paralysis caused by his injuries.

Moushira interrupted her thoughts. "This whole story sounds like a fairy tale. You shouldn't take any of it seriously. There's no reason for you to overthink the situation, because you shouldn't be thinking about a patient that way just because he expressed his admiration. If he truly loves you, I advise you not to pay him much attention. Feelings alone don't cause that much trouble, but acting upon them is usually catastrophic."

24

I woke up to an excruciating headache taking over. My vision was cloudy at first, then gradually became clearer. I was sitting on a chair with both my arms and feet tied—not with a regular chain, but something that was somehow attached to the chair in a way I didn't understand. Shadia too was bound next to me, but she hadn't woken up yet. We were sitting in the main hall of the shelter, while the outer door remained open. I examined the place and noticed two individuals standing by the door in a military stance.

A woman entered. She seemed to be of a higher ranking than they were, and she was followed by two shaven-head guards, one of whom was female. The first woman possessed the same distinctive features that all the rest of her people did. Her curly hair barely went down to her shoulders.

She gave me a sharp look. "I bet you thought you won after what you did."

I stared back at her furiously and tried to untie my arms but to no avail. She moved her hand in a way that warned me it wasn't going to work.

Shadia slowly opened her eyes and looked around in shock. "What happened? Who are those people?"

Before I could respond, the woman strictly ordered us to remain quiet. The woman snapped her fingers and the guard brought a chair and submissively said, "Yes, Ambara."

She sat on it, crossing her legs. "I learned that some idiots interfered with our shared experiment and put strange ideas in your head," she said.

I didn't reply, but Shadia angrily said, "Their idiocy wasn't an excuse for you to kill them."

Ambara ignored her comment. "What did the man who tried to help you escape tell you?"

Before I could open my mouth, Shadia asserted that we weren't going to tell her anything. The woman smiled sarcastically and repeated her question, so I spoke.

"Baldreek said you want to mix our breed, use the Earthlings with yours, the Neanderthals," I said.

Ambara's face changed in an instant. The guard stepped toward me and slapped me hard across the face as Ambara declared, "Don't you dare use that offensive word ever again!"

"What should I call you then?" I asked, annoyed.

"The Earlier Ones, or the Editians. The word you just used carries the inference that Earthlings have been proved superior, as though the Earlier Ones were less advanced human beings." Ambara leaned forward and gazed at us, pursing her big lips and furrowing her slanted brow. She asked once more what information had been revealed.

It occurred to me at that moment that I felt like I was living a dubbed movie. The movement of her lips didn't match the words I was hearing. I almost asked her about it, then I remembered being told that what we were hearing was a result of some strange translation device.

"You want me to inseminate women on your planet, and I think you're here because you want to be the first one in line. Or are you beyond the age of fertility?" I said.

The guard almost slapped me again, but Ambara stopped her with a firm look. She then threatened that she would torture Shadia if I didn't answer her question.

She didn't need to threaten me—I didn't care much whether she knew or didn't. I was just angry at that old hag and her guard, who'd slapped me across the face for no reason.

Shadia opened her mouth before I did. "We'll tell you everything as long as you also tell us the truth—if what they said was a bunch of lies."

Ambara nodded, so Shadia recounted everything Baldreek said. Ambara didn't look satisfied with what she heard, and asked if we saw any tools with them, or if he mentioned any plan, or promised to return.

I said, "We apprised you of everything we know, but you don't appear to believe it."

Ambara proceeded with more questions until she was eventually certain we'd communicated everything. When Shadia asked her for the truth in return, Ambara said, "Many things Baldreek told you are true and some are known by everyone, while other details are just suspicions or conspiracy theories. What can't be denied is that we do intend to go back to Earth, our original planet, and we're going to seize a large portion of a specific region. Its population currently consists of around 300 million Earthlings."

I curiously inquired what area she referred to, but she refused to answer. Then Shadia asked, "What are you planning on doing with the Earthlings who live on that land? Are you going to exterminate them?"

The woman stood up and glared at her.

"Do you think we're as barbaric as you are? We are people of culture, morals, and a refined religion. We would never commit such massacres. The only reason we endure the troubles of these experiments is that we have to learn the perfect method of handling Earthlings. We will fight whoever stands in our way, and after it ends in your defeat or acceptance, we expect almost half the population to migrate. But that means we will still have to deal with around 150 million Earthlings. They will have to submit to our rules and laws, so we have to study your methods of resistance and your attempts to bend those rules. Experiments are happening on single individuals, or pairs, like you. Some even take place among groups of ten Earthlings. Each experiment has a different purpose."

Shadia began arguing once more, attacking the morals that allowed them to displace people, occupy their lands, and forcefully govern them.

I knew debating with Ambara wasn't going to accomplish anything, especially since I assumed Ambara would just criticize our own history, filled with similar examples. She could have even referred to the present, since all those things were still taking place, and no one was able to stop them.

I interrupted Shadia. "How did you choose us, and what criteria do you follow to pair people, or put them in a group experiment?"

"At first it was random," Ambara said. "We don't have the means to send spies who could report the smallest details in your lives, but our big opportunity arrived when you created means of communication that revealed all the different aspects in your lives. Yet, the most important factor we wanted to study still remained: How do you respond to true difficulties that go beyond the scope of your work and social lives? That's why we experimented on thousands of samples."

It boiled my blood when she referred to us as *samples*.

"You didn't like us calling you *Neanderthals*, but then you proceed to call us *samples*?" I asked her.

"We're the superior species. We have the right to call you whatever we want, but not the other way around. Our ethics require us to be fair, but that doesn't mean we're equal."

"I still don't understand why you want to move to our planet when this one seems perfect," said Shadia. "Can't you just borrow a number of Earthlings for your mating problem, or for solving the lack of telomere issue? You can use our genes without abducting us. Or do you truly believe it's a divine order?"

"It is!" Ambara declared. "Millions fiercely believe and abide by that. But there's another issue: our planet is deteriorating. It goes through a major catastrophe around every 1,000 years that kills more than a third of the population. The upcoming catastrophe is expected to take place in around two centuries, and this time it could lead to our extinction. People on your planet believe we have become extinct, but they don't know that only our ancestors who refused to leave the Earth did. They were the ones brutally killed in massacres carried out by Earthlings."

I opened my mouth in disbelief. *Why is this woman punishing us for something our ancestors committed tens of thousands of years ago?* But I wasn't going to argue with her. I only wanted to know their intentions with me and Shadia, and let the Earthlings and Editians both go to hell.

I was about to ask her what was next, but Shadia impulsively wanted to know why they chose us.

"We pick regular, unmilitary people, not celebrities or superheroes. We choose everyday normal citizens because this is who we chiefly wish to study. Normal Earthlings are known to show outstanding abilities of resistance when they are put under pressure, and we wanted to learn the extent of those abilities." Ambara then directed her words to me.

"All we asked from you was a simple choice—that was the core of the first phase. But you're one of those who decided to think outside of the box when you were about to enter the second phase."

My face went red and I asked her what the second phase was. She didn't answer me, only mysteriously smiling. She looked at the second guard, who got something out of his pocket that resembled a small remote control. He pressed it and we were released from the chairs.

Ambara said, "Do you want to learn the details from me, or the instructions video?" She didn't wait for our answer—it was already clear.

"Direct conversation it is, then." Ambara motioned at the guard again and said, "One of the supervisors of the experiment will explain it to you further."

I lost my temper and almost cursed Ambara in my mind for how casually she was dealing with things. She behaved like we completely accepted the original choice and gave in to the experiment, regardless of our roles in it.

As if she heard my thoughts, she said, "Don't forget that you're the reason for extending your time. The blame falls on you, and only you."

I almost snapped back at her, but Shadia wanted to ask one more question.

Ambara impatiently said, "There could be endless questions, dear. I'm sure you especially know that, since you deal with the most curious and fascinating structure doing what you do."

I looked at her, not understanding what she meant. Shadia suddenly blushed, looking evidently nervous. She avoided any eye contact with me.

The woman noticed. "It seems that there are certain things about Earthlings we will never understand, no matter how much we study or run experiments. I never really understood why she didn't tell you about the nature of her job, Omar, even though you're living on a different planet and you're even about to make such a cute couple."

I still didn't comprehend what Ambara was saying. I turned to Shadia curiously, but the woman proceeded.

"Your companion in this experiment is a neurosurgeon who works with the most complicated structure in the world. She deals with human skulls as smoothly as you fix swimming pools."

I was tongue-tied by the shock and heartbroken at the way our two occupations were compared. The strangest thing I had faced on that island was the exact same situation I couldn't understand all my life. It wasn't the overwhelming flood or the electricity I felt in my heart from a large wolf being punished by its trainer.

They were the lies of a woman who I trusted in a way I had never trusted anyone before.

25

Another younger-looking woman wearing a different costume came in. Her smile was so wide that the corners of her lips almost reached her ears. I was beginning to distinguish between the features of those Neanderthals, or "the Earlier Ones" as they referred to themselves. Ambara, for instance, displayed a broad mouth as well, but it was somewhat narrower than this woman. She didn't talk much—only speaking when she dictated instructions.

"You're going to remain on the island for three years, and there won't be a way out. The length of your stay is a punishment for breaking the rules we mentioned earlier. The shelter will be open, but only as a place for you to reside. There will be no supplies, water, or light sources. You have to be solely responsible for your stay here for the entire three years, without our interference. Just you, nature, and untrained animals: some of which are predatory or poisonous, while others are harmless. It's your responsibility to protect yourselves and heal any injuries with the natural resources available on the island. If you survive these three years, you will be safely returned to Earth.

"You only have the right to ask for help four times throughout your entire stay. It will be simply a momentary involvement for a specific case, not a long-term one. There's a certain button you can press in asking for help, then you will receive assistance immediately. After four times pressing it, you will be out of chances, and the fifth will be a declaration of your lack of success.

"If you submit to a defeat, you will be taken to a facility that follows the procedures of our military research institution, and you will be added to the program that includes all Earthlings who failed in the experiment. This program was designed to add you to our support system, which means you will join a military noncombat unit," she said.

Their system and ours were similar after all. Both recruited defeated parties for their military forces, to work among the conqueror's armies as was done by the Romans, the British, the Turks, and all the conquerors throughout history. I listened to everything with half a brain. If she hadn't provided a booklet that summarized everything she said, I wouldn't have remembered a word. I was too preoccupied with what I recently learned about Shadia.

Why did she lie? Why didn't she truly involve me in any information related to her life until now? Whether we return to Earth or not, what difference will it make if she'd told me the truth? Does she even love me at all, or was she simply caught up in the moment?

I hadn't really determined how I felt toward her up until that point, but I knew I genuinely trusted her. There wasn't the usual doubt or anxiety I felt toward all women—I saw her as an extremely close partner. Like she was a part of me...or in other words, like she was my other half.

It might sound like I overreacted to the news, or that it wasn't really a big deal. Yes, we didn't have a written agreement or even a spoken word about our feelings. We hadn't promised each other anything; we weren't living a love story. It was to me, however, more than all of these combined. We were life-or-death companions who protected each other's backs without expecting anything in return.

Shouldn't there be a minimum amount of trust between us that allows her to tell me who she truly is?

I heard Shadia, in frustration, tell that scientist woman that we were going to lose in any case.

"If we manage to return to Earth, my whole life will be ruined by then. I won't be able to prove where I was! I would lose my job and my family, my sick mother wouldn't have anyone to take care of her, and my niece would be moved from one house to another!"

The woman simply responded, "None of this is our problem. If you want to remain here and join the workforce from day one, all you have to do is say so."

The woman, along with the guards, shortly vacated the room, leaving the two of us alone. Everything disappeared in a matter of seconds and we were alone on the island again. I left Shadia and went back to my room, throwing myself on the bed with an empty brain, as if everything had lost its meaning. My life on that island mirrored my life back on Earth. Even though I conquered many new obstacles and faced unprecedented challenges, my heart was still the same. A lonely, mistrusting heart that beat in a world filled with unimportance, fear, loneliness, and losses. A heart that wanted to experience true love just once before it stopped beating.

The lights went out, except for a small bulb hanging in the corner of the ceiling. They were beginning to execute their cruel, lewd experiment. I remained still, with no intentions in mind. I couldn't even think about what our next step was going to be.

Shadia's knocks on the door interrupted my state of numbness, and her guilty voice called out my name to leave the room.

"Sorry, I don't feel like getting out, Doctor," I said.

She remained quiet and I heard her step away. Seconds later, she returned. "Please, please come out."

I opened the door. I couldn't clearly see her face, but tears were sliding down her cheeks. She stood there like a guilty person who didn't have an excuse to defend themselves with, except a worthless plea. She asked me to forget everything we went through, and treat her the way a man would treat a woman in need.

"I won't justify what I did, because you won't understand," she said. In a tone of voice that was both challenging and in pain, she then added, "We are partners who helped and saved each other. I only ask you to continue this partnership, and that's it."

I agreed, but I asked her to leave me so I could sleep for a while.

"Could you please sleep outside your room? I'm not ready to sleep alone in this strange place," she said.

I wondered to myself who was supposed to sleep on the couch and who was to sleep on the floor. *Do I have to sleep on the floor for her just because I'm a man? Or can she sacrifice her comfort this one time and sleep on the floor?*

I asked her that last question coldly—the way the woman spoke a while before.

She eventually suggested moving the couch next to my bedroom door and letting me sleep on the bed, but leaving the door open. I agreed with the same dryness, but my blood was boiling.

If only she apologized, justified herself, or said anything to make me rethink our situation. Instead she's crying, complaining, and being her old arrogant self. She asks for help, but won't apologize for her lies.

I helped her move the couch and entered my room without uttering a word. I lay on my bed and considered our fate, but mainly thought about her. My feelings toward her changed at least ten times per second. I pitied her, detested her, excused her, blamed her, then excused her once more. I also forgave my heart for trusting her.

I told myself that she wasn't an exception, she was like all women: a professional liar who justified her lies to herself as long as it served her. I was sure she felt that lying was how victims protected themselves, and that men are malicious creatures that she couldn't be honest or well-intentioned with. Then I admitted that my paranoia, which prevented me from falling in love and having kids, was caused by the same kind of thoughts.

I was sleeping on my right side, facing the bedroom door with my back turned against the wall. With my eyes closed, I was trying to fall asleep, but my head was spinning with endless ideas. I suddenly felt Shadia nudging her face into my chest, where she fell asleep in my arms as simply and smoothly as she always did. I surrounded her with my arms and held her the way I'd gotten used to during the previous couple of days. She didn't say anything and I didn't ask, like we'd been a pair of lovers for 1,000 years who fell apart and made up without a word.

I considered talking about it, because I hadn't gotten it out of my system yet. How could things simply go back to the way they used to be? I sighed without saying anything. Shadia began breathing rapidly and started sobbing.

"I'm sorry, Omar!" she wailed. She proceeded to tell me about her past traumatic experiences with men—how she stopped trusting them a long time ago, which made her initially hide the truth from me. "One thing led to another, and I couldn't find the right chance to tell you."

She wept, and even though women's tears could be deceiving, I felt that Shadia genuinely meant them. She said that the only reason she cried so hard was that she was missed me. I couldn't talk, so I didn't reply or say anything, I only held her close as she spoke.

"I didn't understand much of what that woman said. I was too occupied with you and how much your heart will change after what you learned. I was too busy thinking if I can ever fix what she broke between us."

I finally replied and assured her it wasn't a big deal, and that I understood. She kept asking over and over if that was true, promising and swearing that she was never going to lie to me again. Once again I said, "It's okay."

But she wouldn't stop talking, she was saying that we must think about the following day, what our plan was going to be, and what we were going to do.

"Zip your lips and go to sleep," I said in jest, nudging her head to my chest playfully. She let out a genuine laugh and said that she found that expression funny for the first time in her life.

26

A whole week had passed since Zahra last visited Omar and finished her procedure. She gave him her phone number and told him not to hesitate to ask for advice at any time, then promised him another visit after finishing his novel...but without setting a particular date. She didn't sit with him for long on that day, and he felt her unease—an obvious effort to avoid any sort of eye contact. He could almost swear, though, that she wished to spend more time with him, or to express many things that she ended up keeping to herself.

Omar's cousin Sameer paid him an unexpected visit. Rivals since childhood, their competition increased with time as the only two male grandchildren of Hajj Awadallah, Omar's grandfather. There was always some kind of ongoing comparison between them that usually ended in Sameer's favor, so Omar carried a constant grudge. For instance, Omar's father tried to teach him various crafts when he lived under his roof, but Omar failed in nearly all of them, unlike Sameer.

Omar left his village and went to live in Cairo starting his first year of college, one year before his father passed away. Sameer, however, stayed in their village, experimented with several jobs here and there, and eventually began to work in fish farming professionally. Sameer's life gradually improved as he flourished in his job, and people compared him even more to Omar, who had no memorable accomplishments. He possessed nothing but a few pretentious words to show off in front of people, to make himself sound smarter and better educated.

After Omar's father's passing, Sameer attended the three-day funeral ritual. On the fourth day, he offered Omar the opportunity to be a partner in his fish farming project so his business would expand even more. Omar agreed, with the condition that if the project failed, Omar would get a full refund of the money he spent. On the other hand, if the project succeeded, he would accept a much smaller percentage than the normal profit.

Unfortunately, the farm was robbed and they both lost a large sum of money. When Omar asked for his money back, however, Sameer denied their deal. The village elders gathered to judge their case, and of course Omar wasn't satisfied with their judgment. They clearly favored Sameer's side because he was living among them. On that day—more than eight years ago—Omar cut ties with everyone in his village. Many condemned him for that decision, but he never thought he was at fault. Perhaps there might have been a better chance of forgiveness if his partner was someone else other than Sameer, because that relationship particularly embodied a long history of jealousy and mistrust.

This was the third time Sameer visited him in the hospital. Omar felt instant unease for some unknown reason. When Sameer sat down in his hospital room—after he brought in generous gifts and his own son—he proceeded to tell his son long stories about his loving relationship with Omar, and how Sameer considered him his only brother. The son sat there with a wide, yet empty, smile.

The visit lasted almost an hour. Omar was anxious to know the reason behind it and understand why he felt unsettled. Soon enough, Sameer began to talk about Omar's plumbing store. He said that he should be the one running it, instead of leaving its management to strangers who might possibly rob the place. Omar knew that his cousin was the first inheritor in case of his passing, but it hadn't occurred to him that the store would be the reason behind Sameer's visit.

Omar dryly responded, "Don't worry about my store. Some strangers are more trustworthy than family. You can wait until I die, then you can sell the store with the strangers working in it altogether." He was barely able to catch his breath while speaking.

Sameer responded, "May you live a long and vigorous life, brother. Your health matters most, and as for your accusation, I forgive you."

He left the room and his son followed while Omar muttered swear words. He knew the people in his village were divided in how they perceived him. Some said he was conceited and vain for no reason, and others perceived him as unfriendly and antisocial. Very few saw him for what he truly was: lonely, frustrated, and impatient.

His overall feelings toward life hadn't changed, besides for the time he spent with her on the island.

The emptiness in his soul was never filled except during those moments when she slept in his arms. He was scared of confronting her with the truth, then dying afterward, which would leave her with a painful memory of her one true love. At the same time, he was afraid to keep living, trying to remind her of what once was.

Pessimistic about his success, he assumed she would turn him down or accuse him of being delirious. In that case, he'd go back to how he used to be before their experience on the island: scornful, lonely, and bad tempered. On top of that were the physical disfigurements from the burns that would go hand in hand with the scars in his soul.

The foreign doctor visited him. He stood with other doctors in the dressing room, wearing a plastic wrap over his fancy suit, and carefully paid attention to the wounds as they were uncovered. Some were clean, while others were still covered in gangrenous tissue.

The doctor paid extra attention to Omar's case because his wounds looked particularly strange. He asked for photos from the first days after the injury, and after he scrutinized them, he became increasingly confused. The injury itself, and the way it spread over his body, were unprecedented.

The expert doctor was of Arabic origin, so he tried to communicate directly with Omar, using broken Arabic to ask him questions about his burns.

"I don't remember," responded Omar.

The man frowned and said, "Not explaining how you acquired those burns doesn't help us treat you."

Omar, however, didn't add anything to what he just said.

"Fine. Perhaps you have a secret, and you don't want to reveal how you got hurt. That's your right. But for your information, your doctors are doing a wonderful job trying to look after you. I admire the way you are choosing to numb your pain, even though I have some concerns about it for your specific case. I think you need skin allografts,[25] which are unavailable in Egypt and extremely costly, even by European standards. I suggested your doctors perform an immediate grafting surgery. If they manage to find a skin donor, your chances of survival will increase."

"What are my chances of survival if they find a donor, and in case they don't?"

"Your condition isn't as hopeless as you think," the doctor responded. "Additional effort and financial support will assure that your survival is very likely, especially if someone donated their skin for you. In Europe, we have a skin bank that exports to different countries worldwide, but it's very expensive, and shipping it might take a long time, which would make it useless by the time it gets to you."

In a broken accent he tried to explain everything to Omar, and in English he replied to the doctors' questions. Omar shut his eyes and listened to their voices as they considered his case, but he didn't get much of what they said. Suddenly, an unexpected

---

[25] Skin allograft: A skin graft taken from another person (usually a cadaver) to temporarily cover burn wounds in patients suffering from extensive burns.

female voice, warm and confident, grabbed his attention. The voice was introducing its owner to the doctor and her role in treating Omar.

He opened his eyes and stared at Zahra as she discussed his condition with the expert. Omar felt proud as she supported her medical opinion with evidence, persuading the doctor to comprehend and accept her method of treating pain.

In addition to transforming the very core of Omar's personality, Zahra helped change two important details in his life. First, she had made him embrace the notion of sleeping next to someone closely attached to him, and second, he was no longer intimidated by the woman he was with. For the first time in his life, he looked at the woman he loved with pride, and wasn't bothered by her capabilities and strong presence.

***

After the expert left, Zahra sat down beside Omar. "I wanted to visit you today to meet the expert doctor who came to check on your case, but more importantly, I wanted to understand what you've done to me."

She proceeded to speak of a strange accident she was involved in a while back. It affected her entire perception of life and left a hollow gap in her. It couldn't be filled until the moment she met Omar. She consulted with her psychiatrist about it, to figure out why she felt so emotionally attached and comforted by Omar, why his words got stuck in her head, and why she felt as if all their conversations completed previous talks. The more time she spent with him, the more she got the feeling that she'd experienced the same many times in the past.

What she also told her psychiatrist, but not Omar, was that any time she was about to leave him, she felt it was natural for her to kiss him. She didn't tell Omar she saw him in her dreams as the love of her life, her closest friend, and a lover who kissed her under a blue tree and held her close in a cozy bed.

Her psychiatrist said that he might resemble someone from her childhood, or that he probably reminded her of her father or grandfather. But that didn't explain why Omar was also attached to Zahra, or why he burst into tears when she told him she wasn't going to pay him another visit. The psychiatrist claimed the feelings resulted from a lack of affection in Zahra's life, and her loss of it when she thought she'd once found it.

Zahra didn't mention to Omar her psychiatrist's interpretation of her strong feelings of attachment. Her unexpected resonance with his own feelings didn't necessarily indicate that her feelings were true—they only showed her attraction to a long-lost kind of intimacy she'd been missing.

At that moment, Zahra was entirely invested in their conversation. She didn't care about the peeks and glances that fell on them, or about Dr. Hend's flattering words that praised Zahra's kindness for her visit even after she was done with her work. The compliment undeniably carried undertones of curious questions. She only wanted to talk to Omar.

He told her many stories about his early life and his father, who noticed his mediocre learning skills at school and intended to choose a reliable craft for him to learn. Then he could rely on those skills after his potential failure at education.

He recounted his father's constant disappointments in his only son. Omar got kicked out of every job as soon as the storeowner got sick of trying to teach him what was necessary. He mentioned how he bought and read used books during his working hours, which was inevitably followed by beatings due to his repetitive mistakes and lack of focus at work.

He pointed to a scar on his forehead and said that he acquired it when he was helping a mechanic at work. The man beat him in the head because he adjusted a lock nut loosely. His father headed to the mechanic, fought with him, yelled at him, and even threatened to kick him out of the village because of his cruelty to his son. Strangely, that same protective father spent an entire night beating him up only a week before.

"Why? What did you do that time?" Zahra asked.

"Because I hid money given to me at school as a gift. It was only eight pounds, three of which I spent buying books...and I lost the other five. When my father learned about it, he burned all the books to teach me a lesson, then beat me up."

She laughed and said, "I was the pampered child at my house. I did very well at school, and everyone in my family constantly praised me."

"Oh, I haven't told you about the biggest incident yet, when I was working under an electrician!" said Omar. "I was reading at the store—as usual—and I sold an extremely expensive tool but accidentally forgot to take the money. The storeowner didn't believe me, of course. He insisted I stole the money, so he went to my father and asked him for it. My father wouldn't accept the accusation, insisting that I was raised too well to commit such a thing. He gave him the money and said that I made a mistake, but I wasn't a thief. My dad walked back to the store and I went home with him, feeling proud to be supported by him. I didn't know what was awaiting me at home."

She laughed at how he recounted the story, how he described the details and the repercussions of his mistakes. It seemed he was no longer in physical pain, ready to go back home at any time. He told her that if he died right then, he wouldn't feel any sadness or regret. He wouldn't feel like he wasted any of his time, because an hour by her side was enough for him to die at peace.

"But why?" Her voice barely came out of her. "I feel like I'm going crazy, like there's a missing puzzle piece I still can't find." Tears welled up in her eyes. She asked him about Shadia, because the romantic words in the story shared between her and Omar felt real to Zahra, and not at all fictitious.

"Sometimes I reread the parts that contain their intimate times over and over, as if I'm reliving moments I experienced myself. Everything Shadia did is what I would do if I was in her place...other than, of course, sleeping in a stranger's arms."

He reached out his hand and squeezed hers. She didn't pull it back that time. She let him take it, but was still overwhelmed and at loss as to why. Her eyes stared at him with a mixture of astonishment and confusion; her lips softly trembled and cold beads of sweat covered her forehead. The hospital room, with all its devices, furniture, and curtains, all vanished in her eyes, as did the doctors, nurses, and the rest of the patients. The walls were replaced with leafy trees, a riverbed, and a waterfall, where only they existed.

He kissed her hand. She snapped out of it and pulled her hand away. In a panicky voice she asked, "Why did you just do that? Who are you?!"

He asked her to keep looking into his eyes. "Contemplate the sincerity of my tears and inspect my chest. Forget it is covered in bandages and try to remember me as much as you can. Reflect on what is between the lines of my story—try to find yourself in Shadia's words. Think about her intelligence, insecurities, and demeanor. Can you connect the dots and visualize the full picture of Shadia? Analyze it well and you will eventually realize that you've been looking in a mirror all along. Zahra, you are the woman who was taken from your house to occupy a chamber in my heart, and presented in the lines of my story."

27

Nearly a month went by after those twisted Neanderthal bastards came and then vanished into thin air. Surprisingly, life wasn't bad at all. In fact, I could say that Shadia and I found a lot of joy and comfort.

For the first couple of days, I left her in the shelter and went out by myself to give her a chance to heal completely. I returned with fruits and water from the nearby stream. I also succeeded twice to hunt small game to eat. Shortly after those days, she began to roam with me in the forest. Sometimes we sat by the riverbed; other times we returned to our shelter and talked all night.

During that month, Shadia recounted the smallest details of her life, evidently trying to make up for the truth she once hid. She told me about the obstacles she faced with her job when she first started, how she challenged and stood up to her colleagues and subordinates, how she tried to appease and defer to her conceited professors who didn't think she fit being a surgeon in general, and especially a neurosurgeon.

"Numerous times I burst into tears alone in offices, recovery rooms, bathrooms, or any place where no one could witness my fragility or vulnerability. You are the first man to see my tears, other than my deceased father, and you are the first man whose chest I've slept on since I was born."

The first time I told her I loved her, we were on the beach. We'd decided to spend that day between enjoying the sea water and grilling meat. Earlier she gathered a collection of leaves and spices that gave the meat a better taste.

The animal I intended to hunt that day looked like a mixture of a he-goat and a caribou, but it boasted sharp and forked antlers. When it spotted me, it widened its stance challengingly and pawed its hooves on the ground. I asked Shadia to stand far away as the animal prepared to attack me.

It charged, directing its horns at my torso. Right before it reached me, I slid to the side and hit it with the cattle prod, but it didn't work for some reason. I shook it and tried it once more, but it wouldn't function.

After the animal passed by, it stood under a nearby tree, glaring at me and rubbing its antlers against the tree branch as if the fact that I avoided its attack made its horns itch. I grabbed my knife to prepare for its next attack, but after it finished rubbing its horns, it simply turned around and walked away.

I heard Shadia sighing and thanking God in relief, but I screamed at the animal. It turned around and stood again, challenging me and pawing the dirt even more aggressively.

We resembled two males fighting for territory. It charged and I ran toward it, then moved to the side again while trying to aim at it with my knife. It was a useless strike: it hurt him, but barely weakened him.

I heard Shadia yelling, "You don't have to be the strong jungle man right now! Let's try for an easier prey!"

The animal turned to face her and began to run, apparently provoked by the sound of her loud voice. I chased it and tried to stab its neck, but to no avail, so I jumped on its back and tried to push it down to the ground.

I was struggling to keep holding it to the ground and asked Shadia to bring me the knife. I was shocked when she rapidly approached and slaughtered the animal easily, like a butcher in a slaughterhouse. It bled to death, repeatedly wriggling until its movements eventually stopped altogether.

We dragged it to the beach together, then I asked her to skin it while I washed away the blood in the water. She refused at first. I smiled and said jokingly, "You're a surgeon. You should be responsible for the tasks that match your job. And you already proved yourself when you slaughtered it so easily!"

I got into the water and drenched myself in it as she watched me. laughing heartily. She skinned the animal with the level of ease of trimming her nails. I eventually got out of the water and approached, still wet, while she muttered comments I couldn't properly hear.

All I could think about was shouting the words "I love you!" out loud. She must have realized something was different because she asked, "What is it? What's wrong?"

I immediately responded, "I love you, Shadia! I love you!"

"I know," she said. "I have heard it many times. I've seen it in your eyes, felt it on your lips, and on your chest when you hold me closely. Your tears have also said it, and that's when my heart felt it the most."

"So, it doesn't matter that I said out loud?"

"Close your eyes. I love you! Did you feel that?" I nodded.

"Okay, keep your eyes closed." She grabbed my hand and gave the palm of my hand a long kiss. "Which one did you feel more?" she asked. "Did your ears understand what your hand didn't?"

I opened my eyes and didn't respond—I just let my gaze wander around her face and take in the kind of love I never imagined to experience.

She was basically speaking in my tongue when she told me she'd never felt as safe as she did with me, that she never let her emotions take over like that, and that she was ready to spend her entire life on the island with me.

Like Adam and Eve, we would marry and have children that occupied our lives on that beautiful island. That was the first time I accepted, maybe even yearned for, the notion of parenthood.

"Will you accept to be my wife on Earth?"

"I accept from this moment, and until our time comes. Do you?"

"I do, queen of the island...and my whole world."

***

We tried to switch up our routine every couple of days, spending one day on the beach, a day by the river, and another by the mountainside. Life was generous and giving, which worried me because I wasn't used to such ease. I expected the Neanderthals to stick to their word and prepare a new disaster. Unfortunately, I didn't have to wait for long.

In the middle of one day, we were camping in the forest and set our tent between two large trees. After a meal of grilled fruit, we sat inside the tent to talk. I was resting on her lap, playfully teasing her. I grabbed her face and pulled it closer to kiss her, then she drew it away. Moments later, she leaned forward and kissed me, then squirmed out of my arms. We were two lovers with nothing but time on our hands.

Suddenly we heard a loud noise outside—different creatures shrieking at the same time. When we exited the tent, we were shocked to see a large number of animals running in our direction, seemingly trying to escape some sort of savage beast. Shadia and I clung to a big empty tree. I helped her get up so she could climb and sit on the nearest branch. I was attempting to jump up when one of my legs hit an animal with a rough shell, so I fell to the ground.

Heavy smoke spread in the air and the birds were flying in the identical direction that the animals ran in, escaping the same trouble. Shadia was waving at me to climb, but I felt that wasn't the right decision. It seemed a better idea to run in the same direction as well. My instincts were proven accurate when I spotted a goat on fire and running. As it dashed along, the flames were transmitted to the dry tree branches.

I helped Shadia down from the tree while animals continued to charge ahead frantically, only now some of them were on fire too. We started running, but instead of following the animals easterly, we ran south toward our shelter. At the time, it appeared to be the best idea, but when we got close to the shelter, the fire blocked our access.

Shadia commented, "We're lucky, because if we'd entered it, we would be suffocated by now."

We changed our direction and joined the exodus, an enormous cluster of various creatures. Everything that moved on all fours ran along with us, except for the birds and some monkeys that swiftly, yet lightly, swung from one tree to another. We were short of breath; we had almost forgotten about the forecasted trials and sufferings. We had both been living like two lovebirds on an isolated island.

How strange that fire is! What is its purpose? Maybe our captors want to burn down all the resources on the island so we will have to press the survival button anytime we want to eat. But if they wanted such an easy defeat, then why did they go through the trouble of conducting the experiment in the first place?

We had almost reached the shore when Shadia stumbled, so I sat beside her as the wildlife passed by. After a while, the animals stopped coming and the fire apparently decelerated. It was no longer near us, but the smoke still lingered, causing coughing and making our eyes itch.

I helped Shadia rise so we could walk to the shore and catch some fresh air. The beach was close enough to almost see. The animals all rested together, carnivores mixed with herbivores in perfect harmony. None of them tried to hunt or fight with each other, as if they knew they were all undergoing the same affliction. Apparently they possessed some sort of moral law that dictated peace in similar circumstances.

We sat by the shore near the forest until we suddenly glimpsed a projectile flying above our heads, heading toward the sea. We heard a banging roar as our eyes followed it, and then we witnessed a great battle.

28

A missile exploded, crashing against another missile shot out of a different craft, one that looked like the ship we nearly escaped in. There were three flying vehicles overall: the central one was at the front: the smallest, with a tiny launch pad extending from its main body. Projectiles were hurled from there to destroy the ones shot from the island. Two other ships were at its back, one on its right and the other on its left. Each was almost double the size of the first one in the middle.

We stood in our places, wondering whether these new visitors came to save us, or if they had a different purpose in mind. The hysterical animals ran left and right, but we remained frozen, overwhelmed with fear and potential hope—which we both wished wouldn't turn out to be false. A large missile fired from the ship on the right flew toward the forest in the direction of the mountain, while the left-hand vehicle began to descend nearby. Missiles were still being shot from the island, met by the ones emitted from the smallest ship.

We heard a massive explosion coming from the mountain's direction, followed by the appearance of several individuals who jumped down from one of the bigger ships. They wore tight black clothes and helmets that covered their faces and shone under the sun. Two of them came near, gesturing that we should join them, while the other two took up defensive stances on the sides. We stood still, stuck in our places. We were overwhelmed, with no idea what was about to happen.

"Come on! You can't waste time," one of the nearing men said.

"Where are we going?" I asked.

He responded impatiently. "Do you want to stay here forever?"

I almost said yes; during the previous couple of days, my life felt like paradise, being rewarded for all the good deeds I did on Earth.

"We're not moving until you say where you're taking us!" Shadia said sharply, and I agreed with her. Before the man could reply, shots were fired from our right. A group of people advanced, aiming at the team that was trying to help us escape.

The two gangs started fighting each other while the first man shouted at Shadia and me to head to the ship, but I still refused. Part of my resistance was because the female scientist from before specifically warned that if we tried to escape, like we once attempted, we would be imprisoned for life.

Irritated, the man shouted again while his followers formed a barrier that protected us from our attackers. We both, nonetheless, insisted on staying. The forest continued to burn and its smoke was taking over the shore. If we persisted in refusing, we would be forced to start over in the middle of ruins where we couldn't live our lives. Yet, I still wasn't too sure of what to do.

The activists who tried to help us the first time were amateurs, just regular folks who tried to make a difference with limited resources. This new group, however, resembled a militia, with advanced weapons and trained members. Maybe they were citizens of a different country on that planet, and we simply got stuck in the middle of a war, or at least a military intelligence battle between the two countries?

All of those conflicting thoughts came out of a brain that no longer knew what was going on. The only thing I knew for sure was my love and devotion for Shadia. Everyone seemed to be aware of that by then, because moments later, the second person shouted at us to move. Then he used a strange-looking weapon—one that looked like an iron knuckle, which are sometimes used in fistfights—and directed it at one of the attackers and shot him with it. He then pointed it at Shadia's head and said, "My job here is to save you and get you out of here alive. If you don't move right now, I will kill her!"

My instincts were right: those people didn't have our best interests at heart. We were only part of their mission—another experiment or plan that we didn't know about yet. *Shadia and I are nothing but mere samples, or two digits in an equation. To be more precise, I am the sample; she is just one of the factors.*

After experiencing the most fascinating feelings we'd ever known, when I was the only man and she the only woman on the island, we were once more returning to being two puppets in a plan that no one knew when was going to end. Adam and Eve were getting kicked out of Paradise and being thrown into the wilderness.

We ran to the ship hovering over the beach with the two men, while the group continued to exchange missiles with the attackers. The aggressors began to retreat when they realized that the two lab rats were secure. We climbed up a dangling ladder, followed by the two men, who physically pushed us to hurry up. We finally entered the ship and sat on the two nearest chairs. The men entered immediately after, followed by two more, then the door was closed and the vehicle started to move.

The walls were transparent, allowing us to see the view outside. The rest of the men got into the other ship. Some of them were injured, but they eventually managed to defeat their attackers, drag along the wounded ones, and enter the second craft.

Our ship hovered above the water, with nothing but the horizon in front of our eyes: the skies, the water, and a series of islands behind us. Our island was in the center, with smoke rising from the burning trees. It began getting smaller and smaller, like seeing the land drop out of your sight the higher a plane went, while your eyes clung onto what remained from its image until it completely disappeared.

The people's faces were revealed after they took off their helmets. They were similar-looking men and women, with similar-looking noses, lips, and foreheads. Only the eyes looked different from person to person, and if it weren't for a slight prominence in the chest area, I wouldn't be able to differentiate between the men and the women.

They all sat in complete silence. It was like being surrounded by wax figures in an absurd museum, one that depicted prehistoric humans wearing sci-fi costumes. Shadia sat next to me in silence, staring into the horizon, like she was a wax figure herself, but at least she was a piece with familiar-looking features. I held her hand to provide her with a feeling of safety and kissed it, but she remained looking the other way.

I was certain that her head also spun with endless ideas and questions, and I knew she was heartbroken over the paradise we both just lost. I asked her not to be afraid and she simply nodded.

"I feel like I just got kicked out of paradise," I said to her.

"But it was fake. We both expected them to do something at any time, and they didn't take their time."

"I think these ones are different," I told her.

She looked at them in contempt spat her words at them: "They're all a bunch of animals."

No one looked at her, as if they didn't hear. She spoke more loudly, trying to get all the disdain and frustration out of her chest in a series of curse words. I never expected a female surgeon to have such a large inappropriate vocabulary. One of them told her to shut up, but she didn't and carried on with her swearing.

Another one then got out a jagged, sharp object, raised it up high, then stuck it in my thigh. We both screamed at the same time. The man coldly said, "If one of you does something, I'll punish the other. I know how much you care for one another."

Our trip continued over the water, which seemed endless. Every once in a while we came across debris. Some of it looked like oil extraction stations, while other masses appeared to be the wreckage of large ships.

After a long time, terrain appeared to our west. I expected the ship to land on it, but we continued moving north. The sun then began to set with beautiful, promising colors that did not match our mood by any means.

When darkness fell, one of the moons appeared to be tiny in the sky and the other one was missing, while a small number of stars presented themselves here and there. A dim light came on in the ship, but the water still extended beneath us endlessly.

The wax figures remained as they were, speechless and unmoving. I asked them about our destination and what they planned to do with us, but I didn't get an answer, so I kept quiet.

Shadia finally rested her head on my shoulder and asked me to never leave her side.

"Why do you think I would?" I asked, but she didn't answer. After some time, she finally spoke.

"If I die now, I will die happy with what we experienced together."

We began to nod off in our seats, whereas the wax figures didn't look either tired or sleepy. I fell asleep without realizing it. When I woke up, Shadia was sleeping deeply on my lap while our captors remained exactly the same way.

As soon as the sun began to rise, I noticed that the sea still extended beneath us. But after few minutes, another piece of terrain appeared, which the ship changed direction to approach. Some high-rise buildings rose from the mainland. The ship gradually declined until it almost came in contact with the surface of the water, then it advanced slower. Shadia woke up and sat up straight, curiously examining the shore and the tall buildings.

The ship stopped moving altogether and its walls became opaque. We could no longer see anything outside except through the glass at the front. I heard loud noises, like the sound of metallic gears moving, followed by a splash against the water. After the ship touched the surface of the water, it dived beneath it and submerged.

The ship, now a submarine, deeply penetrated the water to a depth where the daylight above completely vanished. It smoothly slid forward until we reached what looked like a reef. The vehicle approached rapidly until I got the impression that we were about to crash. A porthole among the rocks abruptly opened and allowed the ship to rush into a tight room. The water drained off, and then the vehicle moved into a metal tube, which fit the ship perfectly.

Inside the conduit, the ship charged ahead at a great speed for several minutes, and it eventually landed in a spacious hall with a tiny slot at its center for our ship. A plump-looking man awaited us, with four guards standing behind him. They wore a uniform similar to the people traveling with us, but didn't wear helmets. All of the guards had shaved heads—both males and females—and they steadily held their positions, whereas the round man advanced with a smile.

The ship opened and we finally got out. The man who threatened to hurt Shadia earlier was the first to exit, seemingly our group's leader. He approached the chubby man, spoke in a bizarre language, and we could tell the man thanked him in return. The rest of the men in our ship then stepped out and followed their leader. The portly man neared us.

"Welcome aboard, our dear friends! I'm terribly sorry about the way you were brought here, but the security on this island is known to be extremely strict, and you're both a bit stubborn yourselves."

We responded to his greeting with numerous questions, to which he laughed and asked us to wait until we could sit down together. He led the way to a small room with a dinner table that contained multiple plates, but no spoons or forks. It was surrounded by four chairs. The three of us sat, then we were joined by a lady. The man introduced her as his daughter.

"Why would you introduce her when we don't even know who you are?" I asked.

The man laughed once more. "I am Anandar, and I run the large institution that was able to get you off the island. We just want to help you."

"Are you among the activists?" I asked.

He replied while chewing a cooked fruit. "Activists? You mean those idiots who think they can change the world? They believe a bunch of myths that were invented by their first leaders."

Anandar grabbed a glass of juice in front of him, drank and loudly burped, then carried on. "We're not pro-authority and we don't support extreme religious notions, but we aren't delusional idiots who call out for a better world. We are investors—we simply want to make money."

My heart sank at his answer. He was denying accusations that, if presented in the right context, might be considered respectable inclinations. He insisted he was only after money, which meant he could justify any wrongdoing to acquire it.

Anandar's daughter seemed to have read my mind, because she interrupted our conversation. "I'm sure that plenty of people on your planet justify crimes in the name of power, religion, or other ideas that may appear to be perfect from outside the circumstances."

While stuffing my mouth with grape-looking fruit that I hadn't seen before on the island, I said, "Yes, but money can lead to bigger problems, including being the motive behind crimes committed in the name of something else."

Shadia glared at me angrily, muttering something regarding all I cared about was filling my mouth with food, and that we didn't have time for my meaningless philosophizing.

"We just want to know what you want from us. What is your plan?" she asked.

Anandar looked at her with a grin. "The lady seems to be a little hot-tempered and impatient. Today you're our guests. You should rest for a while after finishing your food, then we'll finish our talk."

29

Zahra sat on a comfortable velvet chair in her psychiatrist's office. Not knowing exactly where to begin, she decided to try to let everything out. First she appealed to her psychiatrist not to rush into diagnosing her from a box of potential disorders, then base all her actions and feelings on that specific determination.

Her psychiatrist smiled understandingly. She was used to those kinds of requests, especially from patients who happened to work in the medical field. She expected it even more from a neurosurgeon.

Zahra first mentioned Omar's novel, describing how much she was affected by its contents, and how she was specifically touched by scenes that were fueled by romantic emotions. She said she felt physical pain when reading his description of the wolf's bite on the heroine's thigh.

The psychiatrist interrupted. "This is a normal reaction in a woman who's missing a sense of intimacy in her life."

"That's why I asked you to wait until I finish the whole story. Premeditated judgment isn't really suitable here," Zahra said impatiently.

She then continued talking about Omar and her attraction toward him. She described how preoccupied she was with his feelings in a way that didn't make any sense. She didn't understand why she allowed herself to be demoted, in a sense, from her formal status in front of him, and give in to her purely feminine side.

She spoke of being invested in how he looked at her; how the tender touch of his hand filled her small world with meaning and left her in a state of shameless vulnerability. She mentioned that his doctors—and everyone who surrounded him—all looked at her like they knew she was utterly in love with him.

"Listen—" The psychiatrist attempted to speak, but Zahra stopped her again, explaining that the main issue hadn't come up yet.

She finally told her what Omar confronted her with: that she was the same person as the heroine in the novel, and that everything truly did happen between the two of them. It led Zahra to react abruptly, ending the encounter and leaving the hospital as if she were running away from an actual pack of wolves.

As a physician herself, Zahra knew the doctor expected Zahra to subsequently ask about Omar's mental health state, explaining that he was the reason behind this session and not about Zahra herself. That wasn't her aim, though.

"He called me on the phone and told me secrets about my life that no one knew but me, but he claimed I told him those stories myself when we were stuck together on a different planet."

She mentioned that he not only described real events from her life, but also described her own feelings toward people who once played an integral part in her life. He mentioned things she never even dared confront herself with, and crazy ideas that she was too embarrassed to speak out loud. He spoke about her better than how she'd talk about herself.

"The point of this session is that I want you to help me understand one thing: Why do I sometimes find myself believing him, or believing that everything that happens in the novel really did take place?"

"Are you done?" the psychiatrist asked with a kind smile.

Zahra added, "One last thing: I do have scars on my thigh that appeared right after my accident, and I can't remember where exactly they came from."

The doctor nodded understandingly. "You're so invested in Omar's story and his love for you that it's accompanied by an extreme sense of self-condemnation, one that makes you justify everything around you in a way that gives you an excuse to continue the relationship." She paused and leaned forward.

"The man's hallucinating, mixing reality with a story he made up. He probably knew of you a long time ago—maybe you really did treat a relative of his or something of the sort. He liked you, so you embodied the heroine of his story. He became so engrossed in that story that it has become hard from him to differentiate fiction from reality. His honesty about his feelings, originally built upon hallucinations, have convinced you of what he's saying, along with including you in his story."

The psychiatrist justified the scars on Zahra's thigh as an injury sustained in her accident that she didn't remember much of, which was a common result of such trauma. She said the information he knew about her was probably told to him by Zahra herself in previous sessions or phone calls, but Zahra chose to forget saying them because deep down, she wanted to believe in his words.

She explained that Zahra's most personal feelings or emotions were already shared by the vast majority of people, and it happened to match his as well. She compared it to when people read about their zodiac signs and apply it to themselves, fully believing the descriptions are truthful, even though they are a bunch of meaningless, empty lies.

"What if he's saying the truth? What if everything he describes actually took place? The only reasonable explanation for my strong feelings toward him is that I really already have experienced some kind of intimate experience with him, that I knew and loved him before, and now my subconscious is connecting with my emotions despite my memory loss."

"I agree, your subconscious is responsible for the development of your feelings, but for different reasons. Those reasons have to do with your suppressed feelings, the ones you try to conceal in your obsession with your work life."

She analyzed different aspects of the story, trying to convince Zahra that she was merely delusional about her feelings toward Omar—that she didn't truly love him. The doctor even advised her to avoid visiting him and to try to take her mind off that story in any possible way.

The psychiatrist concluded with, "You should take a vacation and travel somewhere far away from all these pressures and conflicts. I'm going to prescribe some medications, and we can set a date for our next session."

***

Zahra left the office with her thoughts scattered all over the place, even though she was leaning toward the psychiatrist's suggestions. On her way back home, she passed the conservatory where her niece Salma took violin lessons. All her life, Zahra yearned to grab a violin and let out all her suppressed emotions through melodies that affected other people as well. She was instead living her dream through Salma, who was like a daughter to her.

Zahra went inside and found the small room where Salma was playing "Lamouni Al Nas."[26] Zahra loved that song, mainly because its melody embraced feelings of sorrow and strong sentiments. It depicted the sadness of a love story that didn't have any logic behind it.

As soon as Salma finished her lesson, she ran to Zahra, who hugged her tightly and proudly listened to her niece's teachers flatter her musical skills. Driving back to the house, Salma suddenly asked her, "Why do you look so distant? Is something bothering you?"

Zahra considered taking Salma out of the country for a one, or maybe two, weeks' vacation. Would it benefit her if she escaped from everything, then returned to a brand-new start? A Parisian conference was scheduled to take place at the beginning of the

---

[26] "Lamouni Al Nas" (in Arabic لاموني الناس): A famous classic Egyptian song.

following month. What if she brought Salma along, skipped the conference's sessions, and instead visited all the major cities in France?

By the time Zahra arrived at her house, she felt much calmer, mainly absorbed with the idea of traveling. She called a friend to ask for advice on the procedure of applying for a visa. Moments later, her phone rang with Dr. Hend's voice on the other end.

"You need to come immediately. Omar is in a terrible state—we need to ventilate him, but he's refusing."

Her heart started racing as soon as she heard the news: Omar's condition had abruptly deteriorated to the extent that he needed a ventilator. Did that mean his time was up? The idea made her blood run cold.

She eventually managed to ask Hend, "Why do you need to put him on a ventilator?"

"Because of severe pneumonia. He needs the ventilator to avoid respiratory failure, but he says that he needs to tell you something before the procedure is done. He evidently thinks he might not survive this complication."

"Why don't you do it despite him?" Zahra said, trying to collect herself.

"It's hospital policy. We need the patient's consent to do this, since he's still conscious."

Zahra felt a lump in her throat as she heard those words. Hend was speaking of Omar's death too casually, which made her eventually decide to grab her car keys and rush to the hospital.

***

Omar was breathing rapidly and shallowly in a way that greatly restricted him from articulating his words. No matter how hard he tried, he was incapable of controlling or slowing down his breath. Each intake of air that entered his chest might have been his very last.

He attempted to take at least one long deep breath that would allow him to talk, but his lungs failed him every time. That was his condition when she finally got to him. The machines connected to his body refused to stop their annoying beepings and buzzings, which indicated the hazardousness of his condition.

Zahra sat next to him, trying to persuade him to allow being put on the ventilator. He tried to emit a laugh, despite the condition of his respiratory system. Then he spoke haltingly and slowly.

"Not refuse ... put on machine ... wanted to see you ... last time ... before I die."

"That's not going to happen!"

"Every patient ... that machine ... died fast."

Her eyes welled up with tears. He extended a shaky hand and rested it on her cheek, struggling to continue speaking.

"Know you'll recall ... everything ... between us ... after I die."

To reassure him, she told him that she already did remember everything, because at that moment, she felt head over heels in love with him. He pulled her face toward him and kissed her cheek with trembling lips. She let him do it despite Dr. Hend's presence, as though his sickness was the excuse behind the kiss, or their love—which was obvious to everyone—was the justification.

He whispered one more request in her ear. "Please ... don't cry ... publish novel. Make sure ... based on true events ... permission to publish."

"You'll get better. You'll finish it and you'll be overwhelmed with its success," she told him. He put his trembling hand under his own pillow and fetched a memory stick, which he gave her.

"This has ... ending ... I love you."

After saying those last three words, he signaled to Hend, telling her to do her job and put him on the ventilator.

Zahra stood in tears as they gave him the sedative, then maneuvered the endotracheal tube into his throat and connected it to the ventilator. She watched his chest regularly go up and down while the buzzing machines silenced, announcing the success of providing his body with sufficient oxygen.

She stood in the corner of the room without trying to conceal her tears any longer. Dr. Hend approached her and held her, reassuring her that he was going to live. She now realized that Zahra was undoubtedly the closest living being to his heart.

30

They made me and Shadia go into two separate small rooms, as they claimed that all their rooms were singles. The rooms resembled prison cells, with a bed that was too small to toss or turn on, a table that could barely handle a cup of tea and a tiny plate, and a narrow bathroom. I sat down and began to anxiously consider the devious things Anandar said earlier.

I tried to sleep. I barely dozed off before one of the armed men entered my room and told me to follow him. I walked behind him in a long corridor without any side doors that eventually led a large hall, one that looked like a conference room. The armed man walked away and left me with chubby Anandar, who accompanied me to a side room in which Shadia and his daughter were waiting.

He sat down and took a sip from a drink that was on the table, inviting us to have a go as well. I carefully tasted the drink at first, then finished the full cup when I liked it.

"I already said this," he said. "All I want from you is one simple favor, as a thank you for taking you out of that island. I'll also take you back to Earth." Shadia attempted to speak but he strictly told her to wait.

"I'm an investor. I paid lots of money, and now it's time to gather my profits, and you'll help me with that, Omar. The upper class in our society is obsessed with the idea of mating with Earthlings. There's a famous black market that works by abducting Earthlings to become samples in that experiment—in agreement with competent authorities, of course. Those Earthlings are then included in a process of artificial insemination to impregnate women who pay tons of money to obtain hybrid babies."

I impatiently looked at him. "Fine, take as much sperm as you want from me, as long as you let us both go as soon as possible."

Shadia glared at me. "Don't forget that the children you're bringing to life are still yours," she said. I told her I didn't have any other option, but she insisted that it didn't make it okay.

"Sweet Shadia," Anandar said with a cunning smile on his face. He waved to the servant to bring him something. "You're both captive here. That's a fact that Omar seems to remember, but not you. Another fact that you both seem to forget is that the extremists in charge will export millions of us to your planet, and your home country could be one of the settlements they choose based on their interpretations of the holy books." His daughter gazed at him in surprise, as if Anandar was announcing a piece of military secrecy, but he assured her that our knowledge of it wasn't going to change anything

"And what about those who refuse to migrate?" Shadia asked.

Anandar sniggered. "They only refuse to make their voters happy when the truth is, each and every one of them is investing in his own field: some in medicine, some in architecture, others in weaponry—people who spend all their time studying the different types of weapons on your planet."

Shadia and I exchanged nervous looks, as it made our hearts sink to learn that those Neanderthals were undoubtedly coming. The man's daughter attempted to underplay his words. She explained that the plans he mentioned were going to be met with great obstacles, and that they were impossible to be executed before a century from now. "Of course there will measures taken to guarantee that the Earthlings won't be greatly affected by our migration, or in reality, our grandchildren's migration."

Anandar interrupted her and directed his words at us. "Think about it well. Either you help us, or you spend the rest of your lives right here." He chose to end the conversation with that firm tone, then he told the guards, "Take dear Omar and Shadia to the room of important guests, and provide them with anything they need."

The guard accompanied us to a large room that looked like a fancy hotel suite, with an extravagant bed in its center, a big table, padded chairs, and a large bathroom. Set up on the table was an elegant dinner and drinks, but we were too overwhelmed with the information we just learned. We sat on the chairs and began to talk.

"Like I said, we don't have a choice," I said. "We can't stay here forever. How can we refuse if we're still captives in this damned place? Plus, what they're asking from us now is much simpler than what others did on the island."

"I don't trust Anandar, or the woman he claims is his daughter. I feel too anxious about all of this, and I need to sleep. I haven't gotten any since we arrived," she said. We got up and I lay on the bed with her, holding her in my arms, but with no desire to sleep.

I softly caressed her hair and back to try to calm her down. She rubbed her head against my chest with her eyes closed and with the hint of a smile, like one you'd see on a child's face.

I kissed her head. She opened her eyes and began to talk.

"I feel jealous. The idea of you giving a part of yourself to those women is unsettling, even if you won't touch them."

"None of this will change the fact that I'm yours. All of me is, including that part. So I'll leave the decision up to you."

She kissed my chest and the palm of my hand, and then whispered with words more touching than Ibn Al Fared's[27] poetry and Al Sonbaty's[28] music. After she finished, she leaned in and kissed me—I drew her head closer to mine. We melted in a long kiss where our heartbeats synced before our breaths did; one that lasted longer than usual. From the fountain that was her lips, I traveled freely among the stars, moving down from the highest hill summits to the flattest plains. I felt like a wandering

---

[27] Ibn Al Fared (in Arabic ابن الفارض): An Arabic Sufi poet (1181–1234).

[28] Al Sonbaty (in Arabic رياض السنباطي): An Egyptian composer and musician (1906–1981).

dervish, one that didn't leave a realm of her body untouched.

The intimacy of the moment escalated intensely. It almost gave us wings to fly with, but it was interrupted when a loud, irritating voice penetrated the stillness of the room. Evidently they suddenly wanted to interrogate us.

I opened the door and saw a coarse-looking guard standing in front of it. She said Anandar wanted to speak to me alone. I asked her to wait, and she ordered me to hurry up. I closed the door, ran to Shadia, kissed her, and told her I wasn't going to be late.

"Take care of yourself," she said. Her tone made me feel like I was about to head to work in the early morning and that she knew my return wasn't guaranteed.

The guard took me back to the room where we all sat together a while earlier. Plump Anandar, the boss, was still there, with another man and a woman.

The boss signaled the woman to speak. "Dear Omar. Anandar didn't get the chance to tell you exactly what's being asked from you. Shadia is too hot-headed, and he was afraid her reaction might affect your decision to accept your mission."

Anandar nodded and the woman stopped talking. He puffed impatiently, then proceeded.

"We're offering a special service to our clients, and that is to conceive an Earthling child naturally." I looked at him in confusion, scratching the back of my head. "We want you to impregnate them yourself, Omar. Is that so hard to understand?"

"I understand... I just don't understand why."

"Because artificial insemination only works once every twenty cases," the woman said.

The other man added, "We used to offer an artificial insemination service, but the women no longer will pay for it because most of the time, the procedure doesn't work. That's why our boss, Anandar, is offering a natural fertilization service at double the price, and we received many requests. Most of them paid a large portion of the fee in advance."

I had gotten used to shocking and humiliating news by then. At that point, I was exactly like my uncle's bull, which people back in my village used to rent to inseminate their cows. No, I couldn't accept that. I decided to fight them as I did on the island, and whatever happened, happened.

"You must be thinking about declining the offer, but trust me, you don't have a choice," Anandar, said, interrupting my thoughts. I looked at him challengingly, and told him I wasn't going to accept even if they threatened or tortured me. "Then poor Shadia will have to suffer...just because her man wants to be a loyal lover," Anandar said.

My mouth filled with saliva that I wanted to spit at him, but he got up from his chair and ordered the other man to continue the conversation because he was required to leave.

A screen on the opposite wall lit up, and the woman said, "What you're seeing right now on the screen is the room that Shadia will reside in—

starting now." It was a small empty room, with only a narrow bed and a small bathroom. It was a dungeon for solitary confinement, like the ones shown in movies.

I felt a lump in my throat as my anxiety escalated. I attempted to speak, but the woman said, "This room can change with only one push of a button, just like this." She pressed something between her thumb and her forefinger, and the room on the screen began to change. The bed and bathroom sank into the ground, making the floor completely flat. The camera zoomed in as sharp pointy spikes rose.

"Imagine your loved one in this room—standing up all night, unable to sleep or sit or rest. If her feet fail her and she falls down from the exhaustion, she'll be pierced by those stakes, causing such excruciating pain that she will be forced to stand up again."

I screamed in anger and lunged to attack her, but the men grabbed me and forcefully sat me down on the chair.

The second man said, "You'll spend the day together and then you'll sleep in two rooms that look like this. She'll go to sleep and you will go do your job. If you refuse to do it, or if the client complains that you mistreated her, your sweetheart will sleep standing on her legs."

I screamed furiously and cursed a blue streak at them, but the man continued to talk while completely ignoring me.

"Not only do our clients want to give birth to hybrid babies, they want a brand-new experience. They're all women with empty lives. They have a lot of blessings, but none of them are satisfactory enough for them. They will brag about your night with them, and it will increase competition within the community. Remember, you're the first Earthling we bringing them, but you won't be the last. So do your job well and we'll take your back to your home with your beloved as soon as our expenses are repaid and we start making a profit."

31

The following day I was taken to a different room with a medical examination table. They asked me to take off all of my clothes, lie on the bed, and wait for the doctor. I was entirely naked except for a small piece of cloth that barely covered my private area.

I sighed in relief when the doctor turned out to be male. He approached me and pressed a button on the side of the table, which caused a screen to extend from it.

The doctor carried a small tool prepared in his hands, which he carefully moved all over my body. The screen produced noises that I assumed to be the sound of my internal organs and blood vessels. I heard the sound of my breath and heartbeat at my chest area, and I heard rumbling sounds from my belly, like when I am hungry.

His exterior work fully finished, the doctor inserted an incense-looking stick inside my mouth for a few seconds, then put another one inside my nose, used two to examine my eyelids, and inserted additional sticks into the rest of my body's orifices.

I completely gave in at that point, like a bride-to-be who was being prepared to forcibly marry a man she couldn't stand. I lost my will to protest. All I had was boredom as I waited for him to finish his dreary task. When done, he left the room.

The image of Shadia standing in that hazardous chamber while trying to sleep standing up made me lose my will to resist.

*Don't pay attention to the humiliating insults in any way. We **will** go back to Earth. We are going to live together, happier than ever. We are going to forget everything that took place on that island and everything about the Neanderthals.*

If they truly were adamant about their migration plan, then it would be our grandchildren's duty to rebel against them. Or rather, the grandchildren of people of other nations. Arabs wouldn't need to fight: we have a long history of brutally fighting conquerors who try to settle on our lands.

I couldn't stop myself from making a silly comparison between what they intended to do and what had already happened with our fellow Arabs in Palestinian lands. In both cases, a group of people found a written divine prophecy that made them expel the current residents, inhabit those lands, and afterward race to convince the world that they had their reasons. They were required to follow their religious verses, they would say, even if it included unjust acts. But at the same time, they managed to ignore other verses.

The Neanderthals are going to take over a country...several countries? Perhaps even an entire continent. The world will fight them, and when they realize warfare won't work, they will have to accept peace. Later, some will even speak up about their rights to return to their original homelands, and that everyone has to accept their presence in the lands they stole.

But then again, what did I have to do with any of these stories and myths? I only had two tasks: the first was to lie to Shadia about the whole thing and claim they only took me to acquire my semen...but I wasn't sure she would ever forgive me if she found out the truth someday.

The second task was to sleep with females who were completely devoid of femininity. I was required to impregnate them and also satisfy their needs. How was I supposed to do that feeling as humiliated and unwilling as I was?

The doctor entered again and informed me that my results were excellent and that I was ready to begin my duties directly. I smiled bitterly, thanked him, and began putting my clothes back on.

Before I was clad in my shirt, he stopped me, got two syringes out from a box, and inserted them in my shoulder one after the other. He said the first shot was responsible for eliminating any chance of infectious diseases, and the second contained supplements that would help me get the job done easier.

He suddenly moved closer and whispered, "Pay attention, Omar! This isn't the headquarters of a company as you'd been told—this is a gang's nest. Most of those people are previous felons, and they won't stop at anything before they get what they want."

I didn't pay much attention. I knew that lots of companies' headquarters were in fact gang nests that traded people's lives for money.

"I want you to know I'm just like you—I'm being forced to do what I'm doing. I'm not some malicious doctor who wants to trade your body for money."

At that moment, I realized their planet included a large variety of people. Just like Earth's inhabitants, some of them were good and some weren't. I thanked him with a smile, so he patted my shoulder and accompanied me outside the clinic, leaving me with my chaperone in a guard's uniform. He took me back to the room, where I was allowed to sit with Shadia. She welcomed me excitedly and asked about the latest updates.

I attempted to speak as casually as possible while trying to avoid eye contact with her curious eyes. "Nothing much. They were just making sure I'm all good, inside out!"

She smiled bitterly and hugged me. "I'm sorry I can't do anything about it. I'm supposed to protect you," she said.

My beloved Shadia, used to going through life on her own without any male figure, felt apologetic because she couldn't do what she felt was necessary to keep harm away from me.

"Do you know why they're keeping us in two separate rooms?" she asked.

Being facetious, I said, "They don't want the two of us to have any interactions that might affect the quality of sperm they'll be getting."

She blushed and attempted to pretend to look serious while asking me to stop joking around and to tell her the real reason. I nervously told her—while still trying to look away—that it was everything I'd been told.

She grabbed my face with both of her hands and fixated her eyes on me. "I don't believe you! I want you to tell me the truth, no matter what." Yet I didn't speak. She beseeched me to open my mouth and say anything, but I looked down instead.

"I'll forgive you for anything except lying to me. We always fix every problem that comes our way—it's been our custom since we first met," she said.

I finally let out the truth about how they intended to torture her. She responded, "Of course they're lying. And even if they're not, I can handle it."

"What if they torture you even worse? What if they rape you?"

"There isn't a big difference between me getting you raped and you getting raped," she said. Her comparison enraged me, so I told her to stop speaking about it and insisted there was a definite difference. She got mad, looked away, and didn't respond.

"They threatened to cut my fingers off if torturing you didn't work. A finger for each day I refuse to do it, and then moving up my arm. In the end, they'll cut off the rest at the shoulder and start on the other side," I told her.

Of course, I wasn't saying the truth, but I was exerting a tremendous amount of effort to sound plausible. She looked at me in disbelief, so I swore to her, "I didn't even consider that possibility. I won't let them torture you in the first place. But if you're okay with them amputating more of my flesh every day, that's up to you."

She welled up and stood in her place, unable to speak. I jokingly asked, "Are you one of those women who say, 'I'd rather he be killed than marry someone else?'"

She chuckled, hugged me, and prayed that nothing bad ever happened to me. "I can't even handle seeing you get pricked by a thorn, let alone what those monsters intend to do."

For the rest of the day, Shadia's face remained grim. She didn't speak much; I tried to humor her, but it didn't work. I apologized again, but she said it wasn't my fault.

For the first time in my life, I felt completely helpless. The woman I loved the most, the breath of fresh air who revived me at my most suffocating moments, was miserable, and I couldn't do anything about it. That feeling tore me apart.

At that moment, I wished to grow wings, like a superhero, so I could hold her tightly in my arms and fly among the stars until her face lit up with a smile. There is nothing in the world more heartbreaking than wanting to put a smile on your loved one's face and failing, no matter how much you're willing to turn everything upside down.

At night, they took her back to her room. She said her goodbyes while whimpering on my shoulder, as if I was being taken away to be hung. They then led me to that large room—the one that almost witnessed our marriage coronation the day before.

The guard who accompanied me laughed and said, "You'll have to kick bad thoughts out of your head if you want to get your job done tonight." I gave him a furious look and sat down to wait.

My client was young. If my evaluation of their ages was accurate, I would assume she was in her late twenties. Her features were less coarse than the others, but she was still unpleasant to my eyes. She dimmed the lights with a press of a remote control in her hand, and with another press, odd-sounding music started playing. I'd never heard anything like that before. It was, however, soothing to the nerves.

Misfortunes at their worst make us laugh, I thought. I felt like I was in an absurd movie, one that switched the roles between men and women. I was sitting on the edge of a bed while a younger woman who paid money to sleep with me was trying to approach me physically.

She sat next to me and whispered, "Let's dance!" I stood up reluctantly, not knowing Neanderthals dance. She moved around me in circles and told me to do the same, then she gradually began to pull closer.

She told me to maintain that same circular dance because they were watching the movement of our bodies on the outside. I was shocked. Why would a wealthy woman who paid a large sum of money allow herself to be filmed? She said that we weren't being filmed exactly, but they noted our bodies' positions using a heat sensor.

I began to question her intentions as she moved backward, still performing her gyrations. She took off her clothes and asked me to do the same, and we continued dancing while she led me back to the bed.

She whispered, "I'm a member of the opposing party. My father's filthy rich; my husband is a famous politician and he wants a hybrid baby. I was the one who insisted on natural means." I swallowed nervously and started to absorb that she was about to justify her horrible act.

"My name's Shawria. I'm going to help free you and Shadia. Right now, try to pretend like we're having sex, or we both will be exposed," she said. She lay close and moved herself and my body around in a strange way. All the time she was explaining what the people on her planet were going through.

"The ruling class is lying to the people. They are all partners in crime, corruption, and oppression who lead privileged lives while millions drown in poverty and suppression. Many even die from hunger and sickness.

"Whole communities are living in the shadows beneath the ground. Most of them don't understand anything and sometimes even accept to be the fuel that drives the battle of powers. The rest of the people are craftsmen and soldiers who live in a never-ending cycle of working day and night. Relentless impediments and challenges assault their daily lives as they try to climb the social bureaucracy of the system.

"Editia's resources are becoming scarce—those in power are depleting them as much as they're exhausting the poor. They promise them a better future and tell them that the way to do that is by using Earthlings and migrating to Earth. Millions of people trust that Earth is their salvation, so they participate in projects that prepare for the 'great migration.' They genuinely believe that their religious obligations compel them to. They suppose we're suffering because we haven't responded to the divine order to migrate to our homeland."

All this time, we proceeded to pretend that we're sleeping together. Shawria stopped moving and explained that her comrades were going to interrupt us at any moment to get us out of there, with the help of Anandar's daughter—a brave girl who played a major and important role in the opposing party.

"Anandar is a leader of an actual gang. He's worked in all kinds of trades, including trafficking humans. Some of the women you are supposed to impregnate are being forced to do so, since artificial insemination didn't work. More than 100 girls are being held captive, some of whom are going to undergo the experiment of bringing hybrid babies to old wealthy men."

32

Shawria continued to explain the master plan while lying on her back. She said that position would make them think we were done, as it was a common posture to increase the chances of fertilization.

She then mentioned that we were going to start moving soon. I immediately responded, "I won't leave without Shadia."

She reassured me. "The doctor will bring her to the ships station."

Shawria said that they were going to help a number of female captives escape as well, as they were the ones who suffered the most throughout this whole process. "The escape plan has been arranged for quite some time. Another Earthling was supposed to be here with you, but they couldn't manage to bring him from the experimenting institution he's being tested at."

What I understood from her was that not everyone was being experimented on the same way. Some were put on islands, like Shadia and me; some were in prison-like institutions and others in deserts or in mazes.

Each Earthling was assigned to an experiment based on the data gathered on their personality by software that accumulated millions of pieces of information about us, mostly through our social media activity. They hacked the phone numbers and electronic devices of the chosen samples, and the rest was executed by programs that our technicians would never be able to unravel.

I felt anxious. With irritable voice I asked, "Is your opposition party truly structured well enough to be capable of overthrowing the rulers and making way for a new regime that doesn't intend to occupy Earth?"

"We are limited in number, but extremely organized. Every day we're joined by new members. A lot of young people—many sons and daughters of the political leaders and the wealthy class—believe in the principles of this revolution. They are the strongest weapon we have in confronting their parents," Shawria said, stressing her words firmly.

I felt like I was speaking to an enthusiastic leftist activist from the sixties. Those young people dreamed of a perfect world, so they carried weapons and fought for freedom all over the world. In the end, nothing was achieved but an epic failure and crimes executed in the name of peace.

The lights went off, and some dim lights flashed repeatedly. She got up, hurriedly put her clothes back on, and asked me to do the same. We opened the door and found the guard standing outside, prohibiting us from leaving.

Shawria sprayed something on his face that made him shriek in pain, then he fell to the ground. She grabbed the weapon on his belt and grabbed it in a way that indicated she'd been professionally trained.

Another guard came running from the corridor, so she swiftly threw a projectile and struck him down. She then stole a small knife from the belt of the first guard and, without blinking twice, cut the skin off his thumb while I followed her around like a lost puppy.

Shawria raced to the second guard and took the same weapon as from the first one. She grabbed my hand and fit the weapon to four of my fingers, adjusting the thumb on the outside. It was too big for me, as those people still had relatively large hands despite having evolved in everything else.

She explained how to use it: "Use your thumb to press there, then with your middle finger, you press to let out a single missile. With your forefinger, you can shoot a missile that creates a small explosion. It can knock two or three people down. But be careful with the latter—you would need training so you can control your aim. Plus, it draws lots of attention…"

We hurried down the corridor and encountered two guards. We both aimed at the same one, which gave the other guard a chance to shoot at Shawria. She shrieked in pain but managed to fire at him.

I checked her injury and saw it was only a shallow wound on her shoulder. Then we rushed along one corridor after the other, while loud noises consecutively went off, which I guessed was their way of sounding an alarm.

We ran into Shadia and the doctor I met before. He carried a weapon in his hand, and so did she. Now she'd become a combatant, which was yet another designation to add to her many titles. I almost forgot we were on a mission, and I was about to rush toward her and kiss every ounce of her body, but

Shawria firmly directed my attention to a guard who was aiming at us and ordered me to fire.

"We're lucky because the guards are too hesitant to shoot you. Come on, that way!" Shawria said. We dashed along the corridors as I held Shadia's hand resolutely. We met another group of guards, so Shawria and the doctor aimed at them: they fell down in defeat.

We headed to the right and proceeded to run for few meters before we reached a group of Neanderthal girls who looked drained and frightened. They were accompanied by an armed man and a woman, whom Shawria and the doctor dispatched.

Our small procession charged toward the parking ditch where our ship landed when we first arrived. Our companions shot projectiles with great skill toward anyone who came our way and anyone who chased us.

The enemies' projectiles knocked down a Neanderthal in our group and one of the female captives. Another was aimed at Shadia but barely touched her scalp before it wounded another girl. Hysteria spread among the rest of the girls and they scattered around aimlessly for a short time.

Moments later, two armed women joined us. They calmed the girls down and adjusted our direction while also managing to defeat the rest of the attackers who came our way. We finally arrived at the ditch, where two ships stood.

The pilot of the first ship was the daughter of Anandar, Profatara. More than twenty girls waited in the large ship. Shadia, the doctor, Shawria, and I headed to the other ship in the back.

Behind the two ships were two vehicles that resembled flying motorbikes. On each one, two people sat with weapons. At the same moment the engines of the two ships started working, we were ready to move in the midst of flying projectiles.

The assailants weren't able to use their explosive missiles because I was in one ship and Anandar's daughter, Profatara, sat in the other. They had to aim at our defenders and the ships' running operations.

When the ships didn't move, Shadia and I exchanged nervous glances. The doctor stared at the tube through which our ship passed when we first arrived, only in the opposite direction. When I asked him what we were waiting for, he said for the power source—then we could go.

As we waited anxiously, a missile struck one of the two motorcycles, with two people riding on it. Shawria jumped out of the ship and fired several explosive projectiles at different attackers, using two weapons in each hand at the same time.

This created an uproar of shouts in a language I didn't understand. The lights suddenly lit up all at once and the ships swiftly rushed through the tube, followed by the remaining motorcycle bike.

The doctor raised his hand, yelling in triumph. "This is a well-thought-out operation. It'll make everyone know that our party is powerful and that it can beat the masters of crime!" He was clapping when he noticed that the woman was staring into the void with tears in her eyes.

"Was he knocked down?" the doctor asked. She nodded without speaking while tears streamed down her face. Shadia patted her shoulder comfortingly. Grateful for her kindness, she said, "He's the one who made me join the opposing party in the first place. I intended to spend the rest of my life with him, and I just lost him to some missile."

Then I understood her rage, and why she jumped off the ship and fired all those projectiles at the people who shot her loved one.

We were still moving inside the tube at that point, but before the ship could finally exit, we suddenly and abruptly stopped.

The doctor said, "They must have cut the power off in the tunnel so their men can block the exit and make us fall into the monster's trap."

I knew he was referring to the burdens of the encumbrances heaped upon the people, so I anxiously inquired about our next step. He told me not to worry because secret supporters were among the technicians in the gang's headquarters.

As time slowly passed, the doctor explained more background. "Anandar kidnaps people like me, as well as other technicians and craftsmen, and forces them to work for him by threatening them and their families."

"Like the Mafia criminals you have on Earth," Shawria added. I was surprised she knew about them. "I'm the chief operator in one of the main technology centers that oversee Earth-related matters. I have the authority to access your internet and watch everything occurring on your planet."

The ships started to move again. Shawria signaled something at the doctor, so he got out a number of weapons and gave each one of us two. "It's expected that we'll find some assailants at the exit, so you have to be prepared," he told us.

Shawria looked at us. "One of the reasons I joined the opposing party is that I've been watching you, getting to know Earthlings—your stories and your interactions—for a long time. I learned that you're not too different from us. You have the same dreams, same goals, and I realized that there wasn't any moral reason for us to feel we are more superior than you. Nothing gives us the right to rob millions of people of their houses and land."

"What about poverty and oppression? Aren't they the main reasons you joined the opposing party?" I asked.

She said, "Everywhere there is rich and poor, powerful and weak. What our leaders intend to do to your Earth, however, breaks all the laws of the universe. Everyone who joins our party believes the same: they're all against that cursed migration. They are concerned about Earthlings, and they care for our families from unexpected consequences."

The ships finally arrived at the exit of the tunnel, which was a filthy area that resembled underprivileged neighborhoods in Earth's larger cities. Debris on one side, piles of garbage on the other, buildings that were half torn down, and tiny huts. I never imagined another planet would have places that look the same as on Earth.

Shawria was right. We did encounter a number of armed enemy personnel as we arrived, who attacked us from two different angles. Luckily there weren't that many of them, and it didn't take us long to beat them.

After exiting the ships, we rushed along several narrow alleys as people stared at us curiously. They wore shabby clothes, with disheveled hair and dirty faces. Their primitive features resembled pictures of prehistoric humans, unlike our chaperones, whose clothes and hygiene made them look more similar to Earthlings in the future.

After almost thirty minutes of hastening down those alleys, we finally reached a worn-out house that looked anything but safe. We entered the building, which was filled with remnants of old belongings and outdated furniture, carelessly scattered all over the floor.

We entered a room, the floor of which was a secret getaway to a ladder that led us to a large hall. It contained plenty of screens and tablets, and a glass box in a corner that would fit only one person.

A number of armed individuals gave me the impression that this party formed a semimilitary structure. They weren't just a bunch of enthusiastic young activists who raised their banners and protested every now and then.

They sat us down on two chairs while someone led the girls to a side door. I didn't know where it led. Later a scientist, who was apparently responsible for returning us back to Earth, arrived.

He began to explain. "This glass box is a machine similar to the one used to bring you here, but this one has been handmade by our small team."

Needless to say, I felt worried. He made it sound like they were using a kid's toy for real-life combat. He apparently understood my reaction, so he clarified what he meant. "It's not any less competent than their machines. I even added a feature that can enable you to go return to a point close to the one you were kidnapped from."

"You mean time traveling?" Shadia asked.

"Dear Shadia, don't try to apply the rules of physics you have on Earth to any of this. There are many false theories you have that you believe are givens. Simply rest assured that the reversible trip I designed moves through time and place...without any further explanation."

He demonstrated the machine and explained how each one of us was going to enter it, and how we were going to be transported. He provided instructions that we had to follow the moment we arrived. One of the armed women asked him to hurry up, so he quickly added, "One of the potential side effects are memory loss of the events that happened to you on this planet. Your bodies will feel hot before transporting, then you will briefly lose consciousness, and then..." The doctor snapped his fingers. "You'll find yourself in the same location that you were taken from."

After a brief argument, Shadia agreed to go first. She held me tightly, took a step back, and stared deeply into my eyes. "I promise I'll never forget you. Even if I lose the memories of the days we resided together, your love will always live in my heart. It will lead me back to you no matter where you are."

I kissed her and pledged to never forget her either. I promised to follow my heart and find her, even if she forgot me, because I knew that only one look between us was capable of setting off the overflow of love all over again. My eyes welled up when I was saying those words to her. We hugged one last time and our tears caressed one another's hearts, then I gently pushed her toward the transparent box.

As soon as she entered it, it began to shake vigorously, then it was lit by a powerful flash. When the flash faded out, she had disappeared from my sight.

My heart sank and I rushed to enter it after her, but the scientist stopped me. "We have to wait for a bit. The temperature in the machine might burn your body if you enter before it cools down from its previous—"

Before he could finish his sentence, however, we heard missiles being fired on the outside. One of the armed people said that we must get going as soon as possible, so the scientist was forced to agree under the pressure of hearing the missiles firing.

I entered the machine, pressed a button, and felt an unbearable high temperature eating at my skin. Suddenly everything went dark, and when I opened my eyes, it was to the sound of many people around me talking and murmuring...and an ambulance's siren.

I remember a stretcher, an oxygen mask, and thinking to myself, *Shadia! Did she arrive safely, or did she burn just like me? Does she remember me, or did the machine make her forget everything?*

Will I live to hold her again, or will these burns kill me once and for all?

33

The operating room was completely different for Zahra on that day. Not because she was in a different hospital altogether, or because the room contained more or fewer advanced machines, but because she herself was in a different setting.

Zahra lay on the operating table, waiting to fall into unconsciousness induced by anesthesia. She had refused to take a local anesthesia and insisted that she completely lose awareness and learn that the surgery was fully executed and done with as soon as she woke up.

The surgical lighting was too bright and it made her eyes well up, so she asked the nurse to temporarily turn it off. Everyone in the room looked at her with respect...mixed with a sense of pity. Others, however, disapproved her actions. She closed her eyes as her veins took in the dosage of the sedative—a white liquid that made the IV bag look like a milk bottle prepared for a baby.

She gave in to the comforting feeling, the utter calmness that was interrupted by a mask covering her face and a gas invading her nose. She inhaled despite herself, and then... Total darkness.

***

Omar spent five days on the ventilator, and Zahra sat with him on each one of those days for more than six hours. She read novels like *Morning and Evening Talk* by Naguib Mahfouz, *The Wedge* by Khairy Shalabi, and *Time of White Horses* by Ibrahim Nasrallah. They were novels he'd constantly discussed with passion, so she insisted she would read them to him. She knew he could hear her despite being in a state of sleep due to the sedatives he was given to keep his body under the control of the ventilator.

She purchased an extremely expensive antibiotic, one that was only provided in the case of highly resistant bacteria, as well as injections that strengthened his immune system. The doctors didn't mind her interventions in his treatment. They all knew the medications were useful and efficient—they simply weren't available at the hospital.

It even occurred to her to write a Facebook post to draw attention to his case and ask people to pray for him. She thought that if there was a 1 percent chance of truth to his story, then perhaps whoever helped him escape and claimed to scrutinize his social media pages would find out that their machine caused deadly burns. Perhaps they would send the proper, advanced medication to treat him. Even though it was a naïve idea that would probably result in a lot of questions and confusion among her friends—who already didn't understand why she cared that much for that specific patient—she didn't care, in spite of the constant criticism for her daily visits.

On the sixth day, Omar's condition drastically improved so he could finally be separated taken off the ventilator in the evening. In addition, he regained full consciousness. His body was thinner and his breathing was still shallow and rapid, but they were relatively more stable.

Zahra contacted the foreign doctor who visited Omar before and asked the department chief to talk to him, which he hesitantly accepted. The doctor informed them that the only efficient solution for Omar's case was a temporary skin transplant...to put a stop to the constant bleeding of his bodily fluids.

The department chief said, "But sir, you know we don't have skin banks in Egypt."

"I suggest you look for a living donor. In Omar's case, he needs at least two. Doing this could increase his chances to survive."

After ending the phone call, the department chief asked Dr. Sameh to contact Omar's cousin and inform him about it. To their surprise, Sameer showed up and claimed he was ready to donate.

Zahra, who knew their history, was deeply touched to learn his intentions. She remembered the times when Omar told her that blood was thicker than water. He repeatedly expressed conflicted feelings toward Sameer, and explained to her that the reason behind their rocky relationship was Omar's jealousy.

Now in Omar's room, Sameer sympathetically patted his shoulder and said, "In fact, I was the one always jealous of him. Our parents, may their souls rest in peace, were the reason behind that. They always insisted on comparing us to one another."

Zahra announced that she wanted to donate as well, which extremely bothered the department chief.

"This is unacceptable—it's becoming too much." He noticed her reaction to his words and said, "Please forgive me, Dr. Zahra. I'm only telling you this because you're like a daughter to me."

When Omar's cousin Sameer arrived at the hospital, Zahra convinced him to inform the doctors that she was going to donate as well. It was guaranteed to compel them to accept her contribution, since he was a blood relative of the patient. Eventually the head of the department agreed.

Dr. Sameh and Dr. Hend both agreed that it would be better not to tell Omar about Zahra's decision, because they knew he would object to it. They wanted him to improve as quickly as possible, even though both of them somewhat objected to Zahra's decision and motives, regardless of their nature.

On the following day, after getting the proper tests done in the university's hospital, one of her professors called on Zahra. He was the only one who'd supported her throughout her career and truly mentored her.

"I only intervene because I care about you" he began. "I learned you're donating skin to a patient in Alsalam Hospital. I don't believe what I've heard, about you being romantically involved with that man, but you still shouldn't do such a thing."

"Thank you for your concern, but I know what I'm doing. I'm a grown woman—not some teenager who does irrational things in the name of love," Zahra responded.

Her professor smiled and said that she'd never spoken to him in that tone before. She fumbled with her words, then politely apologized and asked him to trust her decision, as he always did.

"I'm not planning to worry about a couple of days in bed and very mild post-surgery effects," she said.

Zahra didn't, however, inform her mother or her niece Salma about her plans. She only told them she was going to attend a conference in Luxor for a couple of days.

On the morning of the operation, she didn't visit Omar, but she let him know that she was going to visit him later on that day. The surgery was scheduled to happen at nine in the morning.

The doctors removed a thin layer of skin from her thigh, covered it with bandage, and were swiftly done. Dr. Sameh asked the anesthetist to pay extra attention to sedating her, because the pain in her thigh area would be unbearable.

She woke up to the sound of medical devices, feeling suffocated, as if there were something stuck in her throat. The doctors were loudly speaking to one another, while her throat was spasming.

Her vision blurry, she fell in a state between being unconscious and fully awake. An excruciating pain in her thigh triggered different visions: a wolf digging his fangs into her flesh, Omar grabbing a tree branch and striking the wolf with it, and the wolf on top of Omar, attacking him.

She remembered how Omar lay still while she compressed his chest so he would regain consciousness. She remembered him holding her underneath the trees as she closed her eyes and gave her lips to his while stroking his broad shoulders.

She coughed a couple of times and felt even more suffocated. She saw Omar carrying her above the water level, and she was able to breathe better. She remembered how she stood under the rain, holding on to a tree branch, as Omar was swallowed by the flood's water. When he returned to her, she wept in his arms. She remembered telling him goodbye and entering the glass box, feeling unbearable heat running throughout her body, followed by her loud scream as the tube was removed from her throat. She gratefully repeated, "Thank God."

She lay on a hospital bed in a small room, as morphine controlled her head and filled it with an enjoyable sense of euphoria mixed with the ecstasy brought on by the memories she remembered.

The images were all blurry. She didn't remember where they exactly were or what precisely happened. She only remembered an image here and there, so she submitted to the morphine and the enjoyment of remembering Omar's face as he tenderly devoured her lips...before the image vanished altogether.

At night, she became fully conscious. She asked the doctors if she could go visit him, but they refused, in fear of infection. She repeatedly insisted, however, so they moved her hospital bed to his room and left it right next to his bed.

He looked at her reproachingly. She could see that it hurt him to see her lying on her back in pain, and even more to know that he was the reason. She said, "Your sleeping beauty is awake, and she remembers her prince now."

He twitched in excitement, trying to sit up, so she asked him not to move so he wouldn't ruin the skin grafts. He impatiently asked her how she remembered.

"I'm not sure. If the doctors were to believe our story, they'd say that the pain in my thigh, with the lack of oxygen that heightened the adrenaline in my brain, worked together to activate memories that were related to my current pain. But I would beg to differ: I think it's my reward for going through the operation for you."

Their two beds were side by side, with her feet level with his head and vice versa, which meant they saw each other while talking, like two lovers in a park sitting on opposite benches.

***

They talk for an hour or two before the doctors wheel Shadia back to her room in spite of her protests. In a matter of days, layers of her own skin will attach to his body. This, along with Sameer's skin donation, created a drastic improvement in his condition.

Ten days later he went into the operating room to replace the donated surfaces with skin of his own. Zahra accompanied him in fear while praying that the surgery succeeded. At the time, however, she still suffered from physical pain herself.

Luckily the surgery—the first in a series to graft his burns completely—went well. Before the third operation, Zahra was at work when she found a large package waiting for her. Her secretary said, "A man in a formal suit brought this a while before you got here. He looked kind of strange, like an ape somehow."

Zahra opened the package and found a box inside it, one that looked like a Parker pen set box. She opened it and found two odd-looking syringes and a carefully folded letter:

> DEAR ZAHRA,
>
> I APOLOGIZE FOR WHAT HAPPENED TO OMAR, AND FOR SENDING THIS TO YOU AS LATE AS I AM. WE'RE GOING THROUGH EXTREMELY TOUGH TIMES HERE, BUT WE'RE FIGHTING TO UPGRADE THE VALUE OF HUMAN LIFE, REGARDLESS OF THEIR KIND, ORIGIN, AND NATION. WE'RE FIGHTING FOR A BETTER FUTURE FOR OUR GRANDCHILDREN—AND YOURS.
>
> GIVE OMAR THE TWO INJECTIONS ON HIS UPPER SHOULDER, ONE TODAY AND ONE IN A WEEK, AND HE WILL HAVE A SPEEDY RECOVERY.
>
> I PROMISE TO TRY TO RECONNECT SOON.

She was now sure she wasn't hallucinating; everything that happened to the two of them was undoubtedly real. She wondered whether she should give Omar the medication, which she never heard of and didn't know its benefits or side effects, or wait for him to improve naturally. After considering it for some time, she asked a friend of hers who worked in a renowned laboratory to try to analyze the components of the injection before giving it to him.

The next day, she went to the hospital. When she asked for Omar, they let her know he was in the dressing room. She waited for him on a chair in his room until she was surprised by an unexpected touch of a hand stroking her shoulder. She turned around and saw Omar, for the first time since the accident standing upright and looking at her with a smile. The janitor was positioned right next to him. Zahra stood as well, eagerly faced him, and talked about his upcoming discharge from the hospital enthusiastically. She also told him about their "friends" who sent them a special package that day.

The janitor said that she was going to leave them to finish cleaning the dressing room and closed the door behind her, leaving the two of them alone. Omar raised his gouged arms slowly; he surrounded her with them and placed a genuine kiss on her cheek. They hugged one another with absolutely no cares in their heads.

Epilogue

Dear Zahra and Omar,

First of all, I hope you both accept our belated words of congratulations on your marriage and your first child together. We hope that she, and her children to come, will live in a peaceful safe world.

It's been five years since you were abducted to our planet. Shortly after you left, we managed to liberate other Earthlings and helped them safely return to their homelands, until the government disrupted all our efforts and destroyed the transportation machines we'd produced, but we are still content with the results we achieved. Most escapees regained their memories—they fully remember what happened to them and they all realize the imminent, soaring threat flying over our and your heads.

We made many trials to try to improve the current situation on our planet. After being joined by a large number of supporters, we came out to the public. We openly protested, we exposed many secret conspiracies, we authenticated them with proof, and we spread that information among everyone.

We announced our rebellion and our intentions to prohibit migration to planet Earth. Our biggest mistake was revealing our feelings and demanding a vote on the topic of migration so that the public could decide on it.

Even though we revealed facts about those in power and their secret motives, the stronger party in the system was the so-called religious extremists. Their excuse behind migration was the prophecy mentioned in the holy books, one that predicted that all males were eventually going to become sterile, and that meant we must go back to our original planet.

We didn't question their faith. We only tried to use their reasons to convince people of our own claims. We proved that the holy scripts are flexible and can be interpreted in a number of ways. We pointed out that the lands they intend to emigrate to and settle on—the areas they claim to be holy—don't match the sections where the Earthlings found our ancestors' remains.

We also raised arguments regarding the nonreligious party in power. Our main point was that since our scientists have discovered alternative ways to mate with Earthlings, we can mix your chromosomes with ours through genetic therapy. It will take a lot of research to apply it, but it is still better to resort to that solution instead of the horrendous notion of group migration and conquest.

Our strongest card, however, was revealing that most of those in power, be they religious or nonreligious parties, are going to make tremendous profits from that migration. We clarified that money is the main motive behind dedicating a great amount of resources to achieve the emigration. If those same resources were dedicated to scientific research, we could definitely find simpler solutions.

And finally, we called once more for an inclusive voting system, one that depended on the public's wishes instead of simply relying on our current system, where only those in power are allowed to vote.

After tremendous effort on our part, they responded and organized a referendum, like the ones you have on your planet. Unfortunately, it only allowed certain classes to vote, but not others. When it came time to cast a ballot, those in power prepared their banners and horns.

They eventually managed to brainwash the public that we were barely able to come up with real facts. In the end, we lost fatally when they revealed the voting results. Afterward, they terminated our activities and imprisoned many of us.

In all honesty, we're no well-intentioned angels ourselves. We don't act out of sympathy with the Earthlings only—we're mainly scared about our people. We're scared that their dreams, hopes, and beliefs are being used to create revenue for greedy, relentless people. We're scared of the consequences of moving to a new place, with a new atmosphere and a new land. And if I'm being completely honest, we're terrified of you, Earthlings.

You're a smarter and more resourceful species. Before all the experiments were run on Earthlings, your race seemed gullible and naïve. We've found you're much more brutal. Throughout all of our history, incidents or events that were as horrifying as the ones you experienced just don't exist.

Our leaders are relying on the great technical advances we have over you, but they forget—or at least are pretending to forget—that you learn fast, and that you will find methods to fight us back and knock us down.

What we ask of you, and the rest of the Earthlings we helped escape, is to help us defeat their plans of migration. We will support you with the means and tools you need to resist and fight the invaders. Only you can limit their movements and prohibit this experiment from spreading. After they are certain that their plans will fail, they will swiftly return to Editia.

Your country, Egypt, is scheduled to be among the first lands to be occupied. They intend to occupy about six countries that form a strip on the eastern Mediterranean coast to a depth that will reach, on certain lands, up to 300 kilometers. (No one knows why they determined that specific distance.) But they announced that those were the borders of the lands from which our ancestors migrated.

I know for a fact that you will have your doubts about the contents of this letter; you may accuse us of pretending to be angels who dehumanize everyone else. You might believe that our providing you with the weapons to resist the invaders might have ulterior motives. You might even think that this is all part of a new experiment, but days to come will reassure you that we have the best intentions at heart.

This letter is the first in a series of notes to come. We apologize for this primitive way of communication, but emails are easy to unravel.

You and the rest of our Earthling companions are the only hope for your people, because you're the only ones who can fight against that dystopian future. Please keep these letters secret. Write back, if you want to at the available mailbox address shown below.

We wish you a wonderful life and a future free of fear and pain.

Signed,
Your friends

Author Biography

Serag Monier is an Egyptian award-winning novelist, a plastic surgeon, and a lecturer in medical school. He has four published novels in Arabic.

His last novel, *A New Tale of Andalus*, won the Sheikh Rashid bin Hamad Al-Sharqi Creativity Award in February 2020.

Printed in Great Britain
by Amazon